Raindrop Girl

By AC Williams

Kirsty's affinity with the rain made
her strange in most people's eyes...
until the day she meets Ethan,
owner and boss of the company
housed in an atmospheric and
haunted castle, complete with its
own Grey Lady apparition.
What mysteries will she be
drawn into... and will she also
be drawn into Ethan's arms?

My Weekly Pocket Novels

◆ **Romantic** ◆ **Thrilling** ◆ **Dramatic**

Pocket Novels are quick, easy reads
Fits in your handbag or pocket
Favourite, much loved authors

On Sale Every Fortnight

About The Author

"I wrote my first Rain story in
Sydney aged 13. Since then,
60 short stories have sold
to Australian/British national
magazines. I still love writing the
stories when my lovely characters
whisper to me."
acwilliams-author.com

DC THOMSON
MEDIA

Distributed by Frontline Ltd, Stuart House, St John's St, Peterborough, Cambridgeshire PE1 5DD. Tel: +44 (0) 1733 555161. Website: www.frontlinedistribution.co.uk

EXPORT DISTRIBUTION (excluding AU and NZ) Seymour Distribution Ltd, 2 East Poultry Avenue, London EC1A 9PT Tel: +44(0)20 7429 4000 Fax: +44(0)20 7429 4001 Website: www.seymour.co.uk

Published in Great Britain by DC Thomson & Co. Ltd., 185 Fleet Street, London EC4A 2HS

CHAPTER 1

Yesterday was a day when it rained forever. It was absolutely fantastic sitting outside in my back garden watching the deluge soaking everything. Of course that included me, but I didn't mind. I sat contentedly as silver rivulets cascaded from the leaves onto the grass. I loved the rain and I told it how much every day. The trouble was the clouds didn't always hear my tiny voice. This was the first decent downpour in months.

There was something about the sound of raindrops; as though they were alive. As I tried to get to sleep, they sounded like someone singing a lullaby, splashing against the windows of my home. In a weird way, I imagined that they are talking back to me, describing the adventures they had experienced in the skies up above.

Yeah, yesterday was definitely great. It was upsetting to hear of the floods in Wales on the morning news, especially the part regarding the predicted five more days of continued deluges. Hopefully, things would change soon.

Starting work this morning, I felt rejuvenated. I believed that I was ready for anything. And then Miserable Moira stormed up to my desk.

"Where's that analysis of the Anderson account, November? I need them now!"

"But you only asked for them last thing on Wednesday and I was on a flexi-day yesterday," I stammered. "I've just begun to collate them."

"Not my fault if you take time off. You should have worked late on Wednesday, shouldn't you? Well, shouldn't you?"

I was ready to make a comment concerning

7

unpaid overtime and perhaps if she were able to organise herself better, then I remembered I was on my final warning. I gazed at the floor. "Yes. I'm sorry, Ms Bedford. I'll do them straight away."

"Make sure you do, young lady. I want them before I have my hair done at lunchtime."

"Big date?" I inquired, without thinking. Her icy stare and comments about minding my own business, confirmed my guess. Miserable Moira on a date? I felt sorry for her would-be partner.

After that, the day went from bad to super flipping disastrous. I worked through to lunch and grabbed a sandwich from the canteen, ate it quickly and headed out to the gardens surrounding the Castle and tasteful Annexe. It was spotting once again and I knew I'll explode if I didn't get outside. At least relaxing in the rain showers helped calm me, so I darted across the grass to the bench overlooking the Lake. Working here with that harridan, Moira blinking Bedford, was becoming quite intolerable.

The wooden bench was sopping from earlier yet I didn't care. I stopped and stared back up at the first-floor offices of Transudes Annexe. How much longer could I stay there? Finding another job would be difficult in this uncertain financial climate and there was no one else to support me. No parents, no boyfriend, not even a housemate.

Facing away from Tillymoor, I sat on the bench overlooking the vast Lake of Mists. At least, that was its name. Not Misty Lake, as though that description wasn't grand enough. The guy that built Tillymoor had chosen to construct a lake. It was ostensibly to show his power over nature as the so-called castle demonstrated his power over men and women alike.

There was a maze too, a massive one beyond

the parking lot and weaving around to the rear on the Lake. It was a sign of opulence, a diversion for the rich and gentrified to amuse their time exploring. Sadly neglected for years, I'd ventured into the first few feet of the high hedges once out of idle curiosity. Instead of a neatly trimmed privet or laurel, brambles snaked everywhere, intertwined with the rampant other growth. These days a would-be reveller could be lost for days.

Our Castle was a grand manor home with pretensions of grandeur; turrets and ramparts gracing the skyline in a collision of architectural styles over centuries. It was modelled on Cawdor Castle further north in "sunny" Scotland. Whether the Laird of Tillymoor believed (incorrectly) that the history behind the Scottish play, Macbeth, was linked with Cawdor, no one could guess. He was a mediocre Border Laird with aspirations to grander things.

The Lake took years to excavate and fill. It was said to be deep because the Laird wanted to challenge Hades as well as the Heavens with the meaningless lofty towers. As usual, today was no exception for the Lake. The far side vanished into the otherworldly fog that shrouded the far shores. It was always there, mysterious yet eternal, a gateway to who knew where.

The rain was steady now as I relaxed onto the thick wooden slats, threw my head back and gazed into the falling skies. Seated in this spot, with the rain-kissed Lake before me, was my Happy Place.

I enjoyed working in this age-old setting too, although there was the aforementioned female exception. Transudes was a progressive company employing over a thousand people, most of them off-site. That was a shame for them as the locale of our head office was stunning. Tillymore Castle Had been bought by the company on a whim. It was the perfect new base for their operations, close to rail links and cities yet rural enough to be a sanctuary for staff and visitors alike. What better place to invite prospective clients, wine and dine them in the Great Hall, even put them up in one of the lavish suites overnight? It was an indulgence, yet one that paid off. That was until recently, with a series of inexplicable setbacks that suggested things were going belly-up.

I was aware that my so-called working colleagues were watching me surreptitiously from their windows, making snide comments concerning me getting drenched. I wasn't that bothered. None of them were my friends. At least out in the open, under the soaking rains, I was free, I was me. I closed my eyes and leaned back, stretching my arms across the top of the seat on each side. Within moments I sensed the tension being washed away by the gentle showers, rejuvenated both soul and body. The rain drizzled through my hair, streaming down my face onto my sodden clothing.

Even as a little girl, Mum and Dad were worried over my fixation because I refused to come inside when there was a storm that we Border folk called thunder-plumps. Eventually, they accepted it, always making sure I didn't get too cold or sick. Mum used to say that it was cheaper than horse-riding lessons, like my sister had, and if it made me happy then that was OK.

"Just a few minutes, please. Another cloudburst would be lovely," I said quietly.

"You look as if you're enjoying yourself, Miss."

I jumped at the voice from beside me. Rubbing my eyes, I peered up to see a man. He had

10

an umbrella over his head and was wearing a waterproof coat. I recognised him. He also worked in our offices. I'd seen him a few times in passing although I doubted if he'd noticed yours truly.

As for his appearance, he was around ten years older than me, in his mid-thirties. He was a little on the chubby side but these days most of us were. If anything was interesting about him, I would have to say it was his deep brown eyes and his smile. He looked quite dreamy. I was pleased that he was present.

"Actually, I'm having a great time," I replied, nodding towards the large office building behind. "At least I don't have to listen to Miserable Moira wittering on once I'm out of the office."

"Your boss? Let me guess. Moira Bedford? You're in Accounts?"

"Guilty as charged. I'm on my final chance so don't say anything, please," I added, realising the nature of office politics. For all I knew he could be her relation or best buddy. I shuffled forward on the bench. Me and my runaway mouth.

I was conscious of my appearance, dropping my eyes to see if I qualified for the most outstanding woman in a wet t-shirt competition. A sigh of relief. But even then, here I was, a soggy moggy talking to a half-decent looking guy. My ash blonde hair was plastered to my face and paisley blouse.

"I've seen you down here a couple of times. I started at Transudes recently and I was intrigued. Thought you might enjoy my company."

"What? Sitting in the rain?" He nodded. "Okay… but only if you put the umbrella down, take off that coat, and share the experience," I dared him.

"Fair enough! By the way, my name's Ethan."

"Kirsty." I watched as he closed the umbrella

11

and doffed his jacket before gingerly sitting down on my left. He winced as the pools of cool water on the seat soaked into his slacks. At the same time, it began to pour down more heavily and within minutes he was as saturated as I was. We stared at the state of one another and simultaneously burst into laughter. Anyone passing would think we were mad.

"When I came down, I thought you were talking to someone. Mind if I ask who?"

"The rain."

"And does it answer you?"

"Don't be daft. However, it is a great listener. I was... no, it doesn't matter. You undoubtedly think I'm barking already, sitting on this bench."

We remained there in silence for a while, each staring out to the mysterious Lake waters.

"I bet you were a 'splasher' when you were a boy," I eventually said to him.

"Beg your pardon?" he replied, leaning towards me to be heard over the din.

"A 'splasher'! If you saw a puddle did you jump into it or were you a 'walk-arounder'?"

"Oh, definitely a splasher! Funny. I'd forgotten that. Nowadays I'm a walk-arounder, unfortunately, avoiding awkward situations. I'm too cautious."

"Well, I'm still always jumping in, feet first. Gets me into trouble but a leopard can't change her stripes, can she?"

Ethan was ready to correct my mixed metaphor but noted my wry smile. I continued, "What you need is someone to remind you to take a chance now and then."

"Someone like you?"

"Why not? That's why you came over to see me just now. Every other guy in the office avoids me like the bubonic plague but you crossed that line.

Can't you see them all watching us from up there, safe, smug and dry behind their windows?"

Ethan looked up behind us, peering through the hazy rain to the wheat-coloured stone walls of our workplace building. "You know, you're right. Over the past few days, I've been involved with endless interviews. However, they were all the same. Oh sure, they looked different – old, young, men, women – but as I considered their answers, they all blended together like bleating from a flock of sheep. Boring... predictable... telling me whatever they thought I wanted to hear because some interview techniques app said so. The saddest thing was there wasn't one single splasher in the whole group."

He paused, trying to sweep some of the water off his clothing. It was a losing battle.

"I have to include myself with them. I've lost my passion. I'm just another sheep. Baaaa."

Examining him through the downpour, I could sense the frustration that he must have felt; the realisation that he wasn't who he wished to be.

He stared back at me in my bedraggled state. "I felt so disillusioned recently... And then I saw you, happily seated in this disgusting weather... simply being you. Initially, I didn't realise where you worked or who you were. To me, you were the Raindrop Girl. Stupid name. Sorry."

I looked into his eyes. "Raindrop Girl, eh? So that's why you came out to talk to me? To get away from the other sheep?"

"I guess. I don't know myself. Maybe I needed to wash their woolly sameness off me?"

"So! Do you feel better?"

"Don't know about better. Definitely wetter though. Not very dignified considering my position. I'm the new General Manager. Ethan Davis."

13

"Oh, crumbs. I'm sorry! I didn't realise, Mr Davis, sir." Although I'd heard that there'd been an appointment following the tragic death of Mr Jenkins, the accounts department was in the Annexe at the other end from the Castle which housed the management offices.

Both overlooked the Lake of Mists which staff were encouraged to use in their leisure time.

"Been searching for someone to watch my back, a person who understands the company without being one of the 'old guard'. New blood, more than a Personal Assistant but with the ability to see the bigger picture. A Manager rather than a PA with him – or her – reporting solely to me."

"Good luck with that, sir. Anyway, from what I hear the company's been struggling for months. You being appointed might be a rat with a poor sense of direction boarding a sinking ship. No offence, like."

He grinned, struggling with the rivulets of water streaming from his chocolatey-coloured hair.

"I'm aware of those problems but I was hired because of my reputation to use a welding torch to patch the leaks with Transudes." Clever... He'd used my analogy against me. "I guess I'm not your average garden variety rat."

"That's good. I've met my share of ratty type men. If I have another rat in my life, it'd be the death of me." A pause as I considered where I was and with whom. "May I ask where this is going, Mr Davis... sir? Surely not a job interview?"

"It wasn't, but talking to you in this dreadful rain, maybe it is, Miss November. Is that a problem?"

I eyed him through the silvery downpour in the dull September daylight. This was taking on a quite serious note.

14

"I never told you my surname, Mr Davis."

"No, but your colourful Transudes name tag does. The truth is I did ask who you were when I've seen you by the Lake on other inclement days. You're highly regarded in the workplace... your eccentric penchant for rain not so much."

This wasn't a chance meeting then.

He stared closely. Raindrops ran down his forehead and dripped from his eyelashes and his nose. As for me, I tried to maintain a blank expression on my face. It was difficult.

"Look at you, Kirsty. You love the rain. Come on! Get up and tell me all about being a splasher."

"What? Seriously?" I asked.

Ethan nodded.

I kicked off my shoes, walked forward and pretended I'm telling people of this rainy day. I chatted about clouds and rainbows while stamping around then kicking my toes through the puddles. Truthfully, I didn't have to act. I did what I loved. Nevertheless, next time I danced around like this, I should avoid wearing a dress. Some of those splashes ...

He clapped as I took a bow. "That was brilliant. I loved it. You are a natural splasher, Miss November." Then he stood too, turning to gaze at the mystical dots of pitter-patter rain on the Lake water sending miniature ripples to make the surface alive with beauty. Strangely the fog remained inviolate. The brief interlude between management and lowly dogsbody had concluded. Normal status was being resumed.

"Mr Davis. Apologies for your posh clothes and all. You'll be soaking now."

"Don't be. I have a suite in the Castle. I live there. No problems with changing, even in front of the so-called Tillymoor ghost. Not that any

15

sensible person would believe such nonsense in these modern, progressive times."

He was making light of Tillymoor's morbid history and reputation for things that go bump in the night. That reputation was partially responsible for Transudes purchasing all of this estate for a song. People might love to visit haunted castles but living there? Not likely.

"What about you, Miss November?"

"The changing rooms in the staff gym. My home away from home."

Transudes was a caring company to work for. Another reason to avoid incurring Miserable Moira's wrath yet again. We both began walking along the pathway which split to go to the Castle or Annexe. The parting of the ways.

"It was a pleasure to chat, Raindrop Girl. One question if I may?"

I nodded, droplets spraying off me like a dog shaking her wet fur.

"That report on the Nagashima proposal. You wrote that, didn't you?"

Again, a nod, more circumspect this time. I'd given a great deal of thought and effort to that.

"What you suggested will shave two hundred thousand off our original costings without compromising the end result or our successful tender. Well done."

This meeting on the rain-swept grass was a test. And I'd passed. "Thank you, sir."

"Moira Bedford said it was all hers."

"She would," I replied before considering the implications. His smile vanished and he set off towards the Castle, his back to me. "See you around, Miss November," were his parting words.

Whatever was going on, I'd blown it big time. Would I ever learn?

CHAPTER 2

Double crumbs. Mr Davis was playing mind games with me, giving me a boost then dumping me, as my last boyfriend did with his Dear Kirsty text: *It's not you, it's me.* Well, he got that right. It was him, three-timing me as if I were a dizzy plaything. I wasn't. A plaything, that is, for Kyle or Mr Davis.

Perhaps I should say something clever to his parting remark, yell out "Not if I see you first"? But no; that wasn't me.

He was courteous, complimenting my skills within the business. Maybe he'd come down here to eye me up for a promotion, hopefully away from Moira Bedford.

Then I realised.

"That was another test, wasn't it?" I shouted.

A swivelled head, a Cheshire cat grin and a swaggering Steed-style wave of his umbrella as he kept walking. Talk about cheeky!

Who could guess what was happening in his head? Not me, that was for sure. He'd boosted my ego then let slip that Moira had claimed my diligent work as her own. There were two things I might have done then. Well, three. Keep silent (not in my nature), say gracious words such as it was her idea, or speak the truth as I saw it. Short of calling her a female dog, I had expressed my disapproval. I'd said what I thought and stuff the consequences.

And that's exactly what he wanted to hear without overly saying so.

Result. Yea for Kirsty!

Checking my watch, I needed to skedaddle and

get changed. Good thing they had an industrial-strength hairdryer in the Transudes' gym. No need to style my gorgeous locks, fortunately. Ten minutes and I'd be right as rain (so to speak), ready to start the afternoon shift with my Gorgon boss and her snake-like hair.

Amazing what a lunchtime soak and tête-à-tête with the big boss could do for a girl's disposition.

♦　♦　♦　♦

By the time I was back at my desk, the sun was out. I'd been lucky to catch the showers. Not that me and the sun were enemies. In the summer, people were envious of my tan whereas I put it down to my skin being that hue from my mum's Mediterranean ancestry. Either that or rust. The ashen hair and grey eye colour came from elsewhere. As everyone in the family was dark-haired, my curiosity was stirred. A long-distant ancestor perhaps, their recessive genes resurfacing in me.

Moira Bedford had European ancestry too. She looked like a fortyish Gina Lollobrigida, right down to the dated bright lipstick which didn't compliment her at all. Her auburn hair was flouncy, neatly styled and not a Gorgon-type snake in sight. I told her it looked great but her mind was elsewhere.

As I inquired as to the problem her reply was subdued. "Nothing you can help with, November. It's these figures from April. They make no sense, at all."

I peeked over her shoulder at the screen. It was one of our biggest gambles and if it came off, the company would be sitting pretty. If it didn't...? A thousand P45s and visits to the Job Centre.

"Would you prefer me to take a squizz at

them?" I asked. The other staff were busy with the payroll and end of month accounts. Like it or not I was the closest thing Moira had to an off-sider and one who was competent at more than the day-to-day donkey work, especially after Brodie Douglas had gone off without a word.

All of a sudden, my superior became defensive again. "No thank you, Miss November. Management business. I'll get to the bottom of it. You have your own work to get on with."

The brief connection we had was severed although not by her sharp tongue this time. Some other issues were more important.

Eventually, she closed her computer down and advised the office that she had a scheduled meeting with management. She grabbed the file which I'd slaved over all morning, flicked her newly-groomed hair and set off with a typical Moira warning about slacking off in her absence.

It wasn't required. Her staff were professionals whose loyalty was to the company. If anything, her schoolma'am scolding had the opposite effect but she was too disengaged to comprehend that.

Peering out of the modern triple glazed windows, down at the Lake the afternoon sun glistened off the water, a scintillating series of flashing lights. For a moment, I thought I spotted a person out there, dressed in old-fashioned garb. The cloak over her head was uncalled for given the warmth, a light grey against the sun-drenched colours of the gardens and path.

"Wonder what she's doing out there, Erin? A bit over-dressed, don't you think?"

Erin examined the area. "No one there, Kirsty. A trick of the light?"

I was sure I'd seen her but she was gone. "Sorry, Erin. Must be the sun."

19

Another scan of the surroundings revealed no further signs. My imagination running wild? It wouldn't be the first time but today's apparition was as real as the dampness in my hair.

Moira left soon afterwards, presumably to present my report. Fair enough. My conclusions and name were on the final page. I didn't begrudge her taking some kudos for the efforts of her team.

Every now and then, I stole a glance out towards the Lake to see if my vision had returned but was disappointed. I'd read a Georgian romance book last night and my imagination must have plucked a scene of Miss Devereaux promenading around the Lake and superimposed it on my mind. I saw people and objects which weren't there in my early childhood, these years not as often. Hearing mysterious sounds was another 'gift' according to Gran, though I thought of those gifts as curses and usually kept my counsel about them. Today's question to Erin was a reminder not to share my thoughts with colleagues.

Rain was OK to confide in, though. And perhaps Mr Ethan Davis. After all, he was the one who mentioned our haunted Castle.

I wandered over to our staff room for my afternoon break. We used to have to clock on and off under the old regime, making certain that we didn't sneak an extra minute on top of our allocated fifteen. Mr Davis had changed that with an email edict from his office. Two days after his appointment and the draconian clocking on and off was suspended. His was a positive email to all staff, extolling his belief in their dedication and professionalism. A bit of psychology that had achieved his desired result. Most employees went that extra mile and those that failed to initially were told to change their ways by the rest of us.

A pity that Miserable Moira was the old-fashioned sort, pushing with a stick rather than encouraging through praise.

Lianne joined me at the coffee machine. We each chose the same capsules. "No additional strange women wandering the grounds, Kirsty?"

"I'd prefer not to discuss it, Lianne. No offence."

"Fair enough." She waited until her cup was filled, joining me at a table where we sat. Then she reached over to rest her hand on mine. "However, I do believe you saw someone out there. She's called the Grey Lady. A wandering spirit. She's been seen by others over the years. Read about her in an old history of the area my grandad lent me when I started here."

I scoffed, careful not to splutter my mouthful of Mocha. "Ghosts? You're joking right?"

"Just because you're a non-believer, doesn't mean they don't exist. I mean, you talk to clouds."

She was right... sort of. "I didn't realise you'd heard me. And I talk to rain, not clouds." I gave her a sheepish look. Clouds or rain, definitely a moot point.

"Don't get me wrong, Kirsty. You're a mate and you've saved me a few times when Ms Bedford has lost the plot. You're clever, too and they do say that the smartest people are..."

"Loop de lou?" I offered.

Lianne gave a wry grin. "No. A bit eccentric. Talking to things that don't answer back? Anyways, I do that with my boyfriend. Freddy's the quiet sort. Too quiet. Mostly, it's like talking to a brick wall but he's a real neat kisser and the things he does in be–"

"Too much info, Lianne. I'll take your word for

it. At least you have a guy in your life."

We finished our coffees and cleaned our named cups. That was the thing with a group of women; Brodie was a whizz-kid with numbers but he never washed up, using our cups instead when his invariably was dirty. Men, eh? Lianne offered to let me read the book on the castle. I accepted.

Moira Bedford returned to our offices just prior to knocking-off time. Unusually for her, she kept a low profile, immersing herself in what I assumed was that account she'd previously been concerned with. Her brow was furrowed as though she were trying to make sense of the inconsistencies. When I did cast an eye her way she was beavering away, a demented woman pausing momentarily for divine inspiration. On one occasion she noted my attention, gave an embarrassed half-smile, then resumed her task.

"Goodnight, Ms Bedford," I called out, grabbing my coat and sports bag of sodden clothes. Thank goodness for tumble dryers.

She grunted a reply without looking up. I assumed that date of hers was still on but I dared not wish her well with it. As for me, boxed sets of *Sex in the City* would be as close as I got to romance. My relationships seemed doomed to non-events. Not many guys could tolerate my eccentricities, especially the rain thingy.

I decided to wander down to the Lake and surrounding lawns before going to the car park at the rear of the Annexe. It wasn't raining but the water lent a touch of solitude to a complicated day and I needed that. No dipping my feet in though. Gazing at the tranquil waters with evening insects and birds swooping from above would be enough. With the majority of staff gone, maybe that red stag I'd once seen drinking on the side of

22

the tarn would grace me with his presence again.

A shout from behind started me. It was Ethan calling from the steps outside the ornate doors.

"Miss November. I'm glad I caught you. When I tried to ring, Ms Bedford answered saying that you'd left."

"If you want a date, I'm busy tonight, washing my hair," I replied irreverently as we met halfway between Tillymoor Castle and the Lake of Mists.

His quizzical look suggested my joke had gone too far. Him and me, a date? He was far too old and with him being the big boss it was unthinkable. We moved in different circles, me with beer from Lidl's and him champers from Harrods.

"It was my attempt at humour, Mr Davis, sir. Apologies. How may I help you?"

"I wish to talk with you in my office, please. It's work-related so your dinner plans with me must wait until another evening, I'm afraid." He gave a sardonic grin, brightening up his face, Flirting games? Why not? After all, we had shared a special moment earlier.

"Shame," I responded. Accompanying him to the Castle entrance in the Keep, I marvelled at its imposing size. Although I had heard a little of its history, I'd forgotten the details. The past was never my strong point. I preferred the present where my ideas might influence the future. Musty stone places with rusting suits of armour weren't for me. However, I was curious to see the inside and he clearly wished to discuss work with me away from further rain.

Once we entered the entrance hall, I was stunned. I'd visited castles and stately homes in the past with my folks. National Trust places, recreating those days of Lords and Ladies entertaining other landed gentry. However, seeing the decor, I realised that I had made a grave error in my preconceptions. The interior was contemporary and of very high spec. Well it would be, I thought, giving my rear end a mental kick. Transudes were builders, refurbishing the best hotels in the country. They'd clearly done the same at Tillymoor.

As though reading my little mind, Ethan Davis indicated a montage of before and after photos on a grand display upon a wall. "Tillymoor Castle was a virtual ruin when the company purchased it. Over one hundred years of neglect, open to the elements, no one wanting to or able to afford the renovations. It was an indulgence for my father's company to buy it and even they weren't prepared to pay out for everything, at least not yet."

"Your father? You're Kilmain Rhys-Davis's son? Flipping hell!" Maybe I should have said Sir before his name as his father was a Knight of the British Realm.

"I don't advertise that fact and would ask for your discretion, Miss November."

"Certainly. You can count on me. So, if your dad's a Sir what does that make you? A Viscount, Baron? Just wondering..."

He smiled apologetically. "It makes me an Ethan, no one special. Dad's been retired for years, but once things began to go wrong with the company, he asked me to step in."

Although he did not need to tell me all of this, he had. What a kind gesture. Proudly, he continued the tour of the Castle. The ground and first floors were restored to a high standard of accommodation, although a few ceilings were lowered and the windows triple glazed.

"We came to an arrangement with the heritage people. As the roof had partially collapsed and with a bomb hit in WWII, it wasn't practical to do what they might have wanted. In the end, it was an ultimatum. Let it crumble to dust or allow us to save it. " He continued as he led me up the magnificent mahogany staircase which had been lovingly restored. "The Castle has three guest beds and en-suites on that wing, while we use the East wing. There's a kitchen/diner downstairs but my office is up here along with our living accommodation. Bearing in mind the lateness of the hour, we'll forgo the grand tour, Kirsty. As I told you, I want a word concerning a report."

His tone was reserved, non-committal. Worry clouded my mind, even if I hadn't done anything wrong. Guilt was part of my makeup.

"Lead on, Mr Davis." No smart quips, no banter. Just my 'Let's get this over with' reply.

The office was uncluttered and organised. Well, it would be. Spacious with a work area by the window, desk and one of those ergonomic swivel chairs that you could spin around like a carousel, if you so desired. Additional comfortable settees in burgundy faux leather graced the less formal area. A TV and coffee machine on a long antique dresser added that touch of the past to the modern business-like décor.

We headed for the settees. That was promising. A slight easing of the knot in my tummy. Once seated, he passed me the proposal I'd completed this morning, the one Moira was so upset with me not finishing earlier.

"Is this your handiwork, Miss November?" An inquisition… what fun.

"Basically, yes. Ms Bedford told me what you wanted but the research and conclusions are mine. Projections for alternative funding and modified outsourcing too."

"Look at the end and explain why Miss Bedford has signed it off as her analysis."

Moira was making a habit of taking credit for my word. Deja vu all over again. I flipped through the masses of papers in the presentation folder. He was right. There it was in glorious black and white: Moira Bedford, Accounts Manager. Closing it, I bit my tongue to quell the plethora of swear words that filled my mind.

"Maybe I was mistaken on this occasion?" Talk about a weak comment! Then I had a thought. Mr Davis hated sheep. "But if I were you, sir, I'd compare the font on the last page to the others. I use Times New Roman, 12 point. Moira Bedford uses Arial. As I hadn't completed my hard-copy report until just before lunch, might I suggest she only had time to modify the last page?"

"Actually, I came to the same conclusion." He sat back, flexing his fingers in a most relaxed way. "What would you do about the situation if, let's assume, you were her superior rather than a lowly though gorgeous minion? No offence. After all, she took credit for your work on the Nagashima proposal."

"But I'm not–"

He held up a hand to shush me. "Please, Miss November. Indulge an ageing man."

My imagination kicked in. "Ms Bedford does have issues but she's a decent manager and has instituted several brilliant reforms since I've been with her. I believe these were a blip, an attempt to ingratiate herself with the new big boss."

"Hmm. Interesting. Go on, please, Miss November."

"I would have a not-so-quiet word to show her who's boss and such behaviour is unacceptable but I'd keep her on – with a tighter leash. The company needs her talents as it's already lost Brodie Douglas. To recruit someone else then to bring them up to speed…?"

His matter-of-fact reply caught me off guard. "I could promote you to her position?"

I paused, pensively. "Being truthful, that's not a logical solution. You need a trained accountant for the dead-boring stuff. I play at it. An ideas girl, I'm afraid. Why? Are you seriously thinking that?"

Ethan Davis broke into a laugh. It failed to boost my confidence.

"Well, you could at least pretend to be upset, Mister Davis," I pouted.

"Oh, apologies. No, I agree with your insightful analysis. You'd be a disaster in that position. I was thinking of placing you in the role I've been recruiting. My second-in-command, so to speak."

I gasped. "Me! You're pulling my leg, Mr Davis."

"Tempting though that prospect is, I'm quite serious. Please consider my offer overnight. I believe you'll fit my requirements. Here's a job description with base salary and incentives. A company car as well. Better than that thirteen-year-old Escort you presently drive."

I peered at the remuneration package. "How much? I mean, yeah… oh yeah. That's along the lines I was thinking." For the amount he proposed, I'd almost be willing to kiss him as an expression of thanks but that would be unprofessional and wrong. It was best to play it cool. "What?" I asked, seeing him smirk.

"Sorry. I thought you said you wanted to kiss me. That's how it sounded."

Had I whispered my thoughts out loud? It wouldn't have been the first time I did that, especially upon being surprised.

"Hardly, Mr Davis, sir. Must be this old pile of

27

stones making funny noises. If that's all, I should be getting home." Yeah. If that banger of a car started, that is. "Just one question…"

"Only one?" he teased, his coffee-coloured eyes reflecting the setting sunlight.

I pushed my shaking body to stand. "Excuse me, sir, but why me? You don't know a thing about me apart from that I'm…"

"Tapsalteerie?"

The local word meant topsy-turvy. Quite accurate but not terribly flattering.

"I was going to say canty if we're speaking Borderese, Mr Davis. 'Cheerful and energetic'."

He stood with radiant self-assurance, gazing at me intently. "Don't insult either of us, Miss November. You're bright, witty and have an engaging personality. With my proposal, you have an opportunity to shine, achieve your full potential. As for my decisions, please don't assume that I'm vapid enough to choose you for your pleasing appearance. I've researched you and your academic qualifications. Impressive, but I can find others comparable with your IQ. You possess another series of qualities in which I place higher stock – the French call it 'je ne sais quoi' – you possess it and I want it for the company. Consider my offer – then say yes."

We made our way towards the hallway. Ethan Davis had given me much to mull over. A takeaway meal for Kirsty November tonight, I decided. Making dinner with this to consider was too much.

Just then the door opened and a young girl appeared, probably six years old. She was curious about me yet unafraid. "Daddy, dinner's almost ready," she said.

Ethan Davis was a daddy? That explained the

unusual confidence in a child this young.

"Ava, this is Miss November. Say hello, please, Pumpkin."

"Hello, Miss November. You're the Raindrop Girl, aren't you? You're really pretty."

She reached out to shake my hand, I imagined following her father's protocol for manners, then she paused, a guilty expression changing her cherubic features.

"Can I give you a hug, instead?" she said. I glanced at Mr Davis who nodded. Kneeling down, I let her encircle me with her arms and kiss my cheek as she hugged me. When finished she took my hand and led me outside to the staircase. Her father took her other hand as we descended. At the bottom, Mr Davis excused himself, saying he needed to speak with Heather – presumably his wife. He let Ava accompany me to the door to say goodbye as well.

Outside the flood-lamps vied with the sinking sun to dispel the gathering dusk. Through the glass panes of the bespoke arched door, I noticed movement. That grey figure was moving across the grass toward the Lake, walking into the waters as I watched.

Ava shook my arm to get my attention. "What are you staring at, Miss November? The lady with the cape?"

I was astounded. "You see her too?"

She gave me a quizzical look as though I was stupid to ask such a question. "Of course. She's very sad, you realise."

There was no fear, just a matter-of-factness in what she said. And then, she gave me the greatest shock that I could imagine when she added, "There are others here in the Castle, Miss November. One of them is right behind you."

29

I jumped, despite myself, and turned around, eyes wide open. "What the hell?" I gasped. It was less than two yards away.

CHAPTER 3

Mr Davis appeared at that moment, concerned at my outburst. "What's the problem, Miss November? You gave us a start."

I pointed. "The statue there. I didn't notice it. Frightened me. That's all."

Ava was quite apologetic. "Didn't mean to scare her, Daddy. I'm sorry. She was staring at Mrs Grey Lady." Her little finger pointed at the grey stone statue outside which I'd not noticed either. It was facing the Lake. Ava must have mistaken the figure I was intrigued by for the statue. My ghostly apparition was nowhere to be seen now, assuming I had seen it.

"My fault, Ava. I must be tired. Can I have one more hug before I go? Do we have time, Mr Davis?"

He was pleased that I was allaying her sorrow at upsetting me. "Of course. Heather is just doing the gravy."

I knelt and squeezed her tightly as she did me. Another cheek kiss.

"Now one for Daddy." It was embarrassing for us both but we did it for Ava's sake. A pretence with an air kiss, enough to satisfy her.

"Don't forget what I said, Miss November. Think about it over the weekend and we'll have a get-together Monday morning at eleven."

I took another glimpse at the stone knight in medieval armour that had given me that start. How hadn't I noticed it earlier? My sole conclusion was a distraction by the other Grey Lady.

Outside the air was alive with midges, the Castle grounds quiet as the grave and that ever-present mist swirling calmly over the far edge of the Lake and surrounding forest. No one was around as even Moira had departed, presumably for that hot date.

Despite her trying to take credit for my hard work, I felt good that I hadn't proposed she be punished with dismissal. I'd stood by her yet she'd never learn that truth. I'd been offered a new job that would push me to my limits. However, realising that Mr Davis was taking a chance on me was a worry. Flipping heck – I talked to the rain and saw things which weren't there! Not your typical high-flying manager. Would my colleagues accept my new role? Then again, as a manager, should I be concerned with their impressions?

Mr Davis – Ethan – he wasn't bothered when he sat in the rain, at least not by their views. It wasn't arrogance, him being the top dog and all. It was more being self-confident, certain of his inner self. That's what I'd need to be too.

My car stood alone in the gravelled parking area with that maze behind. Mr and Mrs Davis's cars must be elsewhere. The dusking was here. All around, there was movement, the night-time creatures daring to show their bravery in searching for food. Rats were a problem and all employees were encouraged not to leave snack packets outside, even in the bins.

Picking up my pace, I hurried forward, fumbling with my keys to press unlock. This welcoming oasis of serenity had taken on a more sinister ambience as night approached. For the first time since I'd started working here, I felt afraid.

Suddenly a sound from behind, footsteps on

gravel. Turning to investigate in the semi-gloom, I stumbled, thrusting my hands out in front as I fell. Pain shot through me as a sharp stick punctured the ball of my thumb and my skin was cut from sliding over the rough gravel on both knees. Damn! Then I felt a nip in the nape of my neck along with the sound of tiny feet scampering away.

Painfully, I staggered to my feet, half-running the last few yards to the shelter of the car. The bleeding would stop by itself. The splinter of wood came out cleanly but I wasn't hanging around to fix it properly. With the lights turned on, I spun the car around and accelerated out of the empty space. A dark figure was caught momentarily as he darted behind a tree. At least I thought there was someone. My pounding heart didn't slow until I was well away from the Castle.

♦　♦　♦　♦

Reaching home, I patched up the grazes and hole in my hand with stinging disinfectant after checking for dirt and gunge. Then I chose who to tell of the job offer. There was one name at the top, my sister and confidant, Shannon. She didn't live far away and her partner was away tonight.

"Wow, Kirsty. I was thinking of calling you. Fancy coming to ours for a takeaway?"

"No. You come here. You can stay overnight if you want. Serious stuff going down and I need my bestie to talk it through."

"Okey-dokey. Twenty minutes. You order. Indian? Thai?"

"Fish supper with the usual."

"So predictable. I'll grab a bottle, Kirsty."

"Best make it two," I suggested.

"That heavy?"

"Yeah – and before you ask, it's not a man."

"Oh, a woman?" She giggled.

Same old Shannon. "See you soon, sis."

I hung up, giving my local posh chippy a bell before grabbing plates and glasses. The spare room was already made up. Not that Shannon stood on ceremony. Our dispositions and appearance might have been cheese and chalk but we understood one another. Crucially, Shannon was privy to my visions and believed me, unlike Mum and Dad. Mum was the worst, berating me for dwelling on what she called my imaginary friends. It worked – to an extent. The fairies and wood dryads I shared my early life with soon disappeared. Even Mr Redcap, a goblin whose hat was said to be red from the murders he'd witnessed. Not standard children's stuff, but was Red Riding Hood with the grandma-eating wolf any better? Mr Redcap was the last to leave, leaving me just after the Shellycoats and other mischievous Water Sprites.

Since then, Shannon had been caring for me in a way, not wanting schoolchildren to signal me out as 'strange'. It had succeeded but a part of me was always a rebel. So what if I was a Rain Whisperer? It didn't harm anyone. Nevertheless, there was a barrier between me and Mum. I was never a disobedient girl but poor Shannon had been the mediator keeping peace in the family for as long as I could recall.

She arrived, complete with an overnight bag and toothbrush, a few minutes before our highly nutritious meal was delivered. Being a trained nurse, she checked my DIY job on the wounds then applied dressings. "Tetanus up to date?"

"Yes, mother Shannon. You're such a fusspot.

I just tripped, that's all."

A quizzical stare into my eyes before I looked at the floor. Talk about the silent inquest.

"OK, I was spooked. By a real person, this time. Heard his footsteps. Or at least, I think I did. I'd seen a phantom a few minutes earlier. Frustrating, Shannon. Times happen when I can't tell the other world and reality apart. It's... it's getting worse."

"Rubbish. You're the most level-headed woman I know, rain whispering aside. Anyway, Big Sister is ready to keep an eye on you. Always."

We hugged, then she went over to Tibbles to ruffle his fur before letting him return to his dreams of chasing mice through fields of catnip.

Once our meal began, we chatted about her adoption progress and if she and Bruce had been accepted as yet. I couldn't believe the hoops they'd had to jump through but the end was in sight. They wanted a wee lassie. Having children of their own had proved impossible, such a shame for this lovely couple.

Then we each changed, ready for bed, a glass of wine close by as we snuggled up on our respective settees. It was girlie talk-time.

Shannon began with a broadside concerning my choice of night-time attire. "Pink PJs with bunny rabbits on, Kirsty? No wonder your love-life is non-existent."

I laughed at that. "They're comfortable and I do have sexy nighties, Shannon. Admittedly they're covered in cobwebs but they're there, ready for dusting off."

"I damn well hope so. You need someone in your life, a man who's as crackers as you. Tell me, little sis. Why the need to goss tonight?"

The Aussie 'cab sav' wine, as the colonials

34

called it, was already warming my tummy. Confession time. "I spent my lunchtime on a bench near the Castle lake getting soaked with a guy by my side."

"I knew it! There is a man in this world who's as bonkers as you. Continue, little sis."

I took a large sip, steeling my courage. "He's my boss, Ethan Davis. And he's offered me a job in management." There. I'd said it.

Shannon remained quiet, her brow furrowed under her dark brown fringe as she silently pondered away. "Ethan Davis... Ethan Davis? I recognise that name." Like a girl possessed, she sprang from her couch to return in a moment, clutching a magazine. Frantically flipping through the pages, she thrust a double-page spread in front of my face. "Is that him?"

I tried to focus. Too much vino. "Yes. That's him," I gasped sitting up and suddenly sober.

"Wow! Super-wow, sis! He's a celebrity. And he's dead sexy. Did you sit with him talking to the rain, like you usually do? Don't suppose you could get his autograph? For a friend?"

I glared at her long enough for her to realise that she'd overstepped the mark. Contritely, she zippered her lips, poured another glass for us both then sat on her cushions, elbows on knees and leaning forward. Her eyes were fixed on me, staring intently before an exaggerated blink.

I burst out laughing. My sister was as daft as me although in a different way.

"Did you hear me say that Mr Davis offered me a job as his sort-of assistant manager?"

"No way, Kirsty! You accepted, of course. It's a total no-brainer. He must fancy you rotten."

My smile flattened a little. "He's married. Has a daughter, too – Ava – really cute. But all of this

35

pales before what I saw near the Lake – twice."

"I'm not sure I want to hear this, Kirsty. Mum said..." Shannon was trying to downplay my mysterious sightings, as always. The ultimate peace-maker. She'd seen things too as a child yet unlike me, she accepted Mum's insisting that they didn't exist. Then she became Mum's brown-eyed girl and muggins here was not so much shunned but certainly consigned to the reject bin in the factory of life. We hadn't talked in seven years since I left home, I mean really talked. And Dad, being Dad, had sided with Mum.

"A woman, garbed in ancient clothing. Grey and sad. I think she drowned there at the Lake."

Shannon came over to give me a sisterly embrace, making me shift up on the settee so that she could join me.

"Lately, I've sensed strange things too, Kirsty. Maybe thoughts of our daughter awakening the past, I have no idea. But one thing I do understand is that Mum was acting in our best interests as she saw it. I think she was once like you... like us, but she repressed that side of her nature and wanted to change us too."

"Why do you think that, sis?" For my entire life, I thought Mum never believed me, but suddenly, I could understand why she might have done what she did. The flack I had at school, my absence of friends, being called a liar over and over by everyone including teachers. Even in this workplace, I was a pariah of sorts.

"I heard poor Granddad speaking when I last visited her and Dad. Not the words as such, more a feeling he was in the room, telling one of those anecdotes of his... rambling. I swear Mum heard it too. She said 'Dad' and looked over to the seat he always used. But it was our father's reaction that worried me most. He told her to get a grip, laughing it off when she tried to explain. I said nothing but the haunted look in Mum's eyes... It wasn't the first occasion she'd heard it. I haven't been back since."

That made sense in a way. Dad was a quiet type of guy letting Mum appear to be the one wearing the pants, but she wasn't. Far from it. A glance, a single word to remind her to watch herself, occasionally but enough. They loved one another but perhaps when it came to the gifts the females in our house possessed...?

"Maybe you should discuss it with Mum? Or Gran?" she suggested.

"Gran? I don't have her address or number."

"I do. Helps to have clever Bruce, the ultimate computer nerd. He tracked her down. I haven't dared to talk to her yet. Maybe we could go together?"

"Yeah. I'd like that, Shannon."

Far from being the perfect family, ours had more skeletons rattling around than a graveyard. Gran and Granddad on my mother's side had been banned from having contact with Shannon and me since I was eleven. They'd respected my mother's wishes. Furthermore, we girls were not permitted to go to the funeral once our grandfather passed on. We found out a week after the event. It was wrong and was the last straw that caused that final split between me and my parents.

"How about tomorrow, Saturday?"

If I had the feeling that I'd been manoeuvred into this, I didn't object. I'd tried to find her myself without success. Shannon had greater perseverance. We needed to start bridge-building. Shannon went to her bag to retrieve the phone number from a notebook. After toing and froing, I was elected to be the one to call. I was nervous but once prompted, I grabbed my mobile and rang. It never occurred to me that she might not want to talk to us.

A few rings and an irate voice yelled, "I don't want double glazing and I haven't had an accident that needs a bloody solicitor. Now, get lost!"

"Don't hang up, please. It's Kirsty, your granddaughter. I'm with Shannon."

I heard her breathing then a very matter of fact statement, "Kirsty? Shannon? At last. It's about bloody time!"

◆　　◆　　◆　　◆

We arranged to meet for lunch tomorrow as the journey to Ayr would take us an hour and a half each way. For whatever reasons, Mum and Dad had excelled themselves in keeping Shannon and me apart from Gran. Her version of events differed from my parents but I was positive who was telling the truth. Our parents had their reasons but, at this moment, I wasn't interested in hearing them. Shannon felt the same way.

The conversation on the phone was brief yet emotional. As we were on the loudspeaker, Shannon could hear and comment too. Although our dad had forced mum to ban our grandparents from contacting us directly, they'd sent gifts every birthday and Christmas – presents we'd not received.

Although they'd tried to make peace, every entreaty was dismissed. New addresses were kept from us so that even when I tried to track them down, I couldn't. According to Mum, they'd washed their hands of our family, including us. It was heartbreaking to hear. After making arrangements to meet at a restaurant on the seaside, Gran astonished me by suggesting that I must have questions about my special talents.

"How did you guess?" I wondered.

"A dream, Kirsty. Maybe a prophesy if you believe in such things. Danger lies ahead and you must be prepared."

"What sort of danger, Gran?" Shannon asked, her voice alarmed as she grabbed my hand.

"Murder. People are already dead from the wolf's reach and you might be next."

CHAPTER 4

We met at a bijou cafe on The Esplanade, overlooking Ayr Beach. As the day was unseasonably warm, Gran was awaiting us on the terrace. The reunion was loving and embracing and extremely gushy. Shannon had driven over as, in her words, she wouldn't be seen dead in my less than stylish car. I think she was referring to the multi-colours of rust, primer and faded red paint, not that I could blame her.

Maybe I'd drive in my posh new company car when we next meet; that is, if I accepted the position. The more I considered Mr Davis' offer, the better I felt. I'd done assistant managing earlier in my short career but that was with an itsy-bitsy company of thirty employees, south of the border. To me, it was about planning and exploiting the skills of the people already there. Managing people? Yeah. I could do that.

"Let me look at my two big girls," said Gran. She didn't comment on my bandaged hand. As for the knee grazes, they weren't visible under my mint green slacks.

"Not sure that 'girls' is appropriate, these days. And I'm expecting," said Shannon. To be fair, Shannon's olive skin was positively glowing in the sunlight. She and I had never been close sisters, Shannon's dark eyes and hair contrasting with my natural ash-blondness and blue eyes. We were both tall and despite our love of choccie and wine, quite fit in both senses of the word.

My grandmother had hardly altered, silver-grey replacing the chestnut brown I recalled. She was in her late sixties and wasn't the nimble person I recalled from fourteen years ago.

Food and drinks were ordered, all those years of our respective histories condensed into précises, and then it was time for those unspoken truths to claw their way upwards from the shadowy depths of the past. I was the first to broach the subject. Being warned of murders tended to speed the conversation along today,

"Gran. Are we psychic or something? I – we – see and hear things that aren't there."

"Aren't they?" Same old inscrutable Gran, answering a question with another. "Just because others can't experience them, does not mean they don't exist." She waited momentarily, considering an explanation we might accept. A dog being led along the footpath in front paused and twisted her head to the side.

"See her? She hears a sound, a higher frequency than you or Shannon. I can't hear it. Well above the twenty thousand hertz you young-uns can detect. My ears aren't as good now, maybe twelve thousand hertz. I struggle to understand squeaky high-pitched voices. Also, radio waves. We can't detect them but your phone can. Taste and smell? Shannon's sense of smell is far better than yours, isn't it?"

"Yeah, you're right. I always put too much perfume on. People thought I was... well, let's say I used to be propositioned a lot," I confessed. "Don't wear it now."

"Your mother, me, and you two bonnie lasses are gifted to feel aspects of existence that others can't. See that old man on the wooden bench over there?"

Even though I was able to, Shannon struggled until my grandmother laid her hand on my sister's.

"Oh yes," she exclaimed.

"Now check out the other benches. They're all concrete and steel. Wood rots you see."

"Your point, Gran?" Shannon was impatient.

"It's an echo of when he died, a fleeting image that might be a trick of the light or a memory held by the beach: clothes, person, wooden slats, shoes. He's gone now, but in three days or a year, he might reappear to those like us that are attuned to the Earth's energy aura."

She was right. The grey figure on the grey bench had faded into oblivion.

"Damn!" Shannon gasped. "I am a freak after all." She took a gulp of water, draining her glass then refilling it.

Our school taunts and Mum's continuing denials had caused her to deny her talents, me less so. Even then, I wasn't too keen on experiencing the supernatural. Normal living was hard enough. But I might get answers to who Kirsty November truly was, at last.

"Why us, Gran? Genetic mutations? X-Women, like in the comics and movies?"

She giggled at that, a loving sound that I realised I'd missed for far too long. "There's so much you need to find out in such a hurry, especially with that premonition I had," she said,

41

becoming quite serious. "The truth is you two, me, and your mother, we're Poseidon's children. You do understand who Poseidon is, don't you?"

Shannon's education was sorely lacking. "The only Poseidon I've heard of was an upside-down ship movie," she conceded, sheepishly.

"Greek god of the oceans, crown and a dirty great pitchfork. The Romans called him Neptune. Surely, you've heard of him, sis?"

Her reply reeked of mock indignity. "Yes, thank you, dearest Kirsty. I'm not a total dodo."

"Weren't his children mermaids, Gran?"

"Doesn't matter if they are, Kirsty," my gran responded. "Don't fancy a fishy tail, and swimming around all day. No, the term is figurative. We have an affinity to water, especially you, my girl. We draw our energy from it in a way – the rain falling, waves breaking, any movement. That's why I live by the sea."

That sounded intriguing, an explanation for my joy at getting soaked. But energy? I doubted that.

As if sensing our doubts, my grandmother continued, "You lasses have never been allowed to train and achieve anything approaching your full potential and I blame your father for that. I hate to speak ill of anyone but the man has been jealous of your mother's gifts and has done his best to repress hers – yours as well. That's why the big bust-up so long ago. Your mum made me promise never to contact you girls and I agreed to it. But since you contacted me, I'm not breaking any agreements."

We continued to discuss family and heritage quietly as we ate. Gran promised to begin our belated education into all things soggy if we wished. Shannon agreed, possibly concerned for her little one, but me…? The three words: *bring it on* sprang to mind.

We arranged a visit to my place the following weekend, by which time Gran proposed to have answers about this wolf character. I gave her the details of my work and Ethan, all of which she noted down in a small booklet. It was done very professionally yet both Shannon and I couldn't see the point. She was an old woman, without being too rude, now retired and probably content to do knitting or attending Scottish Women's Rural Institute meetings. The highlight of her life might be to make perfect clootie dumplings to finish a Burn's Night supper of haggis, tatties and neeps.

"Excuse us, Gran but what chance have you to unearth any shady background?" Shannon inquired. "You're no Miss Maple Syrup."

"You don't know what your Gramps and me did? Of course, you don't. Your parents wanted us to keep it a secret so as not to upset your 'delicate dispositions'. We sold the business but I keep my hand in… a little, old lady? The perfect disguise." She sat forward, her eyes twinkling with mischief behind her granny glasses. "Miss Marple? Poirot, Sherlock Holmes? They were all rank amateurs compared to us. We once ran the biggest Scottish detective agency this side of Edinburgh. If Transudes have any dirty secrets, I'll root them out!"

◆　　◆　　◆　　◆

I had a great deal to consider back home that night. Plus, the damage to my body from last night was giving me gyp. Meeting Gran after all these years, my strangeness being inherited as well as my future role in an organisation that had danger associated with it. What was that expression? When it rains, it pours? How frighteningly appropriate.

After one of those microwave meals for one that tasted like chopped up cardboard, I chose to grab the last bit of a cheesecake that I'd saved for a special occasion. This was a definite special occasion. With this new job, I'd be in a stronger position financially. My days of struggling to pay the mortgage, rates and insurances would be a thing of the past. Maybe a holiday this year to somewhere more exotic than Benidorm: Greece, cruise, Canada even? Always fancied there.

On impulse, I chose to look up Neptune's children on my laptop. He was a randy so-and-so, fathering what read like hundreds of goddesses and mortals. Several kids were divine, others giants, as well a horse or two. That sounded a bit far fetched. On the other hand, sea nymphs intrigued me a lot. I became distracted by nereids, not strictly speaking Poseidon's children but close to him. They were water spirits, hanging around with the Greek sea god. Even so, they were the products of the Greek's imagination whereas we were real. As Gran said, 'Poseidon's children' was a name, that was all.

On the other hand, Ethan with his backstory was a better person to research. I glossed over his family, Dad being a Knight. I was intrigued by the company he ran and any dodgy connections. Apart from an indication that there was a cash-flow hassle, nothing else seemed untoward.

It was at that point that I realised why I'd thrown myself into computer research tonight. The phantoms, ghosts, ethereal auras, past echoes, spectres – whatever you called them –

they weren't a trick of my imagination any longer. The excuses I used to calm my apprehensions no longer cut it. For whatever reason, my senses were attuned to glimpses into a dimension co-existing with us. More concerning was the idea that right here, right now, there might be the memories of departed people reliving their last moments of life in a non-stop cycle of energy.

Ghost stories frightened most people but not me. Gran explained that they weren't sentient, their soul had gone to a higher realm. "It's like endless reruns of that video you loved to watch as a child, Kirsty. The mermaid one."

I laughed, causing a few people in the Ayr cafe to smile. "Ariel?"

"Yes. No matter how many times we watched her, she never did anything differently."

I'd read once that ghosts colours faded over the years, from a red dress to dark pink then pale colours. Reruns of reruns... nothing lasts forever.

It had been a long day and I was done in. I stood and stretched my arms. "If there are any ghosts around, I'm going to have a shower so please close your eyes until I tell you otherwise," I said to no one in particular. A joke. Although I could accept that spectral beings existed, they couldn't see or react to me. The thought of one walking through a door, clanking chains, turning to me and addressing me by name, that would send me screaming into the streets as much as Ariel saying, "Hi Kirsty. Care to swim with me?"

◆　　◆　　◆　　◆

Although no one worked at Transudes main office on Sunday, I decided to tell Mr Davis my decision in person. He wouldn't mind – at least

I hoped he wouldn't. Maybe Sundays were sacrosanct, a family day with Heather and Ava, a picnic or attending church? If that was the case, I'd leave as soon as, not wanting to intrude.

My impromptu visit wasn't logical yet it was as though I was drawn to the Castle. Was the Grey Lady reaching out to me from her watery grave or was it me, dreaming of that workplace connection we'd shared on Friday? It'd be great to see Ava as well because she reminded me of myself at her age. I trusted Heather wouldn't mind.

The car made it in one piece, however there was a clunking sound that suddenly became worse as I drove through the open metal gates, along the gravel road to Tillymoor. I wasn't an expert but clunking in a car wasn't a good omen. Another reason to accept the job: a company car.

At least I didn't need to announce my arrival by knocking on the door. Ethan Smith was outside in the parking area with another gentleman who was leaving, from the looks of it. He had his door open and was ready to get in when my Chitty-Chitty-Clunk-Clunk drew up not far from them.

"Sounds like you've got big-end problems, Kirsty," Mr Davis observed as I approached.

"That's a bit too personal, Mr Davis. It's no bigger than yours."

He indicated I turn around giving him a better view. I did, swinging my hips provocatively as per his 'cheeky' comment. Then I smoothed my dress down and faced him again.

He broke into a grin. "You're right. If anything, it's a Goldilocks bottom: not too big, not too small. just the right size. Not that I'm an expert."

His guest remained stony-faced. If anything, he ogled me, reproachfully, bushy eyebrows meeting like two hairy caterpillars.

46

"And who is this… this woman, Ethan? One of your tennis floosies, no doubt." His words were as vindictive as his stare. The fun banter was over but I wasn't going to let him win.

Raising my fists and scowling, I said, "One of? You promised there was just me, darling."

"And you are, Kirsty my precious. Scout's honour. Dib, dib, dib." He did a mock salute, scout style, grinning at our continued banter. I did hope Heather wasn't listening. However, he went on, "Kirsty November. This is a… work colleague, Christian Wilczyca."

As Mr Davis didn't elaborate on my position, floosie was my default setting. I narrowed my gaze to the sour-puss guest. "Wilczyca? I believe that word is Polish for wolf." That'd put him in his place. I eyed him carefully. Gran had mentioned a wolf entering my sheltered life.

He was surprised at me recognising that fact. Neither of us had an accent.

"I believe so, Miss November. My ancestry but not my nationality. You seem remarkably well-versed in Polish for a… fluff-bunny?"

"Sir. I'm neither a floosie nor, as you so eloquently express it, a fluff bunny and your continued rudeness do you no favours."

He continued his insults, unperturbed by my statement. "No need to be coy, Miss November. I know you and your sort, gracing the monthly pages of a man's calendar, displayed in your nakedness between Miss October and Miss December." That was extremely cruel, making fun of my name. "But your knowledge of Polish does intrigue me."

A false smile curled my lips, as disarming as I could. The gloves were off. "My family spent three years in Lublin when I was a child. Enough

47

to speak a few words. By the way, Wilczyca is a female wolf. A male wolf is 'basior'. Our secret, I think – unless you'd care to share anything?"

His smug expression was replaced by a face like thunder. Game, set and match to me, I decided as he left without further words or a backward look. No great loss from my viewpoint nor, from Ethan's indifference to the departure, to him, either.

"Remind me never to take you on, Miss November. Actually, I'd prefer to call you Kirsty, if I may. Suddenly Miss November has other... connotations, and I don't want to be distracted by thoughts of you gracing my office wall in the all-together." He blushed. "And please call me Ethan. We are going to be intimately involved, after all – professionally, of course."

"Of course, Ethan. Can't say I thought a great deal of your guest."

"Nor I. A necessary evil as the business makes for strange bedfellows at times." The mention of bed brought another blush to his cheeks. My boss was a right beamer. However, this flirting was getting out of hand. He was married for Heaven's sake! The last thing that I wanted was to become involved in a menage-a-trois, particularly with my boss. We both deserved more than that. Sadly, being around Ethan stirred a long-suppressed passion which I'd need to redress sooner rather than later.

"I assume that you're here to accept my offer. Or did you find me too irresistible to stay away for longer than a day?"

Damn it. He was continuing to flirt. I had to nip this in the bud for both our sakes.

"Just the job, Ethan. I am in a relationship already but thanks for the offer."

A momentary glimpse of disappointment perhaps before a more subdued response. "Very well. I shall discuss your responsibilities and show you your new office. It's not yet furnished. Perhaps you can start officially tomorrow afternoon – short notice and all. Sunday is normally my day with Ava but you're welcome to join us for lunch then a walk round the grounds. My daughter is presently fascinated by insects and all things crawly. Perhaps your childhood hobby might help?"

Hmm. He was aware of that, was he? He'd done his homework big time. And if so, did he realise my being in a relationship was a lie? How much research had he done on his Raindrop Girl before approaching me?

Ethan accompanied me to the Castle entrance in the Keep although he maintained an almost wary eye on the Lake of Mists as if expecting to see someone.

"The ghost of the Mists," I said, thinking aloud.

"I don't believe in the supernatural, Kirsty, in spite of the reputation of Killymoor. My mother was taken in by so-called spiritualists. They destroyed her life. I'd prefer it if you didn't mention ghosts, especially around Ava."

What could I say? "Of course, Ethan." One step forward, two steps back. For the first time, my tenuous belief that I was in tune with spirits had been vindicated by Gran. Now, I was being told in no uncertain terms, to suppress that knowledge. The gap between Ethan and me had widened. I could play by his rules. My future job depended on it. The compromise was… well, disappointing.

I nodded towards the stone statue of the caped and hooded figure. "Who's that supposed to be?"

"From what I've heard, she was the wife of the guy who built Killymoor. Even in life, she wasn't

49

permitted to wear bright colours by her puritanical husband, the Laird who built this place. He erected the statue as a homage to her after she took her own life. She's buried on the far side of the waters in that foggy land that never feels the sun's warmth. Suicide by all accounts although some rumours in written records suggest she was forced to drown herself."

"Ava mentioned that the statue looks sad."

"Yes it does. I might not accept the presence of ghosts but I must confess that there's an ambience permeating Killymoor. That melancholy aura surrounds the Castle once everyone has left for the day. Even I find it disconcerting to be outside. Inside, that's another matter. I'd thought of leaving and renting elsewhere until I saw you out there in the rain. Your happiness… it made me realise that it's people, not buildings, that are important. Possibly you and my family are destined to be here together, although I've no idea why."

That was intriguing. Yet it explained why he'd approached me, asked me to be his Girl Friday. An inexplicable connection?

"I made enquiries and realised that you had qualities which would help Transudes, Kirsty. You are being offered this role purely on your qualifications"

I mopped my brow in an exaggerated show of relief. "Whew! Thank goodness for that. You keep doing that as if you can sense my apprehensions. You're not a mind reader, are you?"

"Of course not. It's simply what I would think if I were in your shoes. Great minds…"

"Think alike," I added, almost tempted to take his hand in a show of understanding. Struggling, I restrained myself. "But you're right. I do feel a connection to this place and may I humbly admit, to you as well. Spooky, but nice spooky."

We reached the large doors and entered, leaving my car forlornly parked outside. I suspected its life was over, that it had given up the ghost, so to speak. I'd phone the breakdown people who'd arrive, shake their heads and take it to the car graveyard. As for me, taxi trips for the foreseeable. It wasn't ten miles from home. Things could be worse. Was it serendipity that I'd be getting this new company car sooner rather than later? I wondered briefly if it would have Transudes plastered on the side of it and a flashing neon sign on top. Hopefully not.

I was certain that the phantom whom I'd witnessed from afar was the same person as depicted in the ancient larger-than-life statue guarding the castle. Being cynical, I decided that the Laird had commissioned it, not as a homage to his wife but in a perverse attempt to keep her tied to this place forever. From what I'd heard, he hated to be cheated from things he desired and her suicide was just that. No wonder he chose to portray her as a subservient woman, forbidden even to smile.

As Ethan had suggested, my morose mood lifted as we entered the Keep. In this ultra-modern reception area, such emotions were almost effrontery. This lovely place felt right and welcoming. We went up the stairs towards the office area.

"My father decided that this derelict ruin needed an inspiring facelift. Although it seems disrespectful in one way, I believe that it achieves the result he wanted. Would you agree, Kirsty?"

"Absolutely. And I'm sure the building agrees."

"You sense it too? I thought it was just me."

51

The ethereal mental connection between us was back. We had differences in attitude yet we had a curious link too.

"It's the energy, Ethan, from the people living and working at Tillymoor. A building, any building, needs a purpose and sheltering people from the elements of nature is important to its soul. Did your workplace predecessor live in the Castle?"

On the first floor landing, Ethan walked to a window overlooking the front. He stared out at the Lake of Mists yet again as though drawn to it and the place I'd seen the spectral figure; the same one he refused to accept.

"No. And our overnight guests have told me they approve of the decor. We've secured more than one contract purely on the achievements here. To take a ruin and transform it in such a spectacular way is a ringing endorsement for us."

Our debate was interrupted by the clatter of tiny footsteps on the grand marble staircase.

"Ava's coming."

I nodded in agreement as Ava appeared, studiously holding the polished wooden bannister as she watched her every footstep. Yet, in place of the immaculately dressed youngster whom I'd met on Friday, she was scruffy, flour-smeared over her pretty red and yellow dress.

"Ava, where have you been?" Ethan was a little distressed and scooped her up to brush aside what he could from her hair.

"Sorry, Daddy. I been helping make a cake."

"Hmm. I can see that now." He ruffled her hair causing a cloud of white dust to float around.

At the same time, I caught a reflection from something shiny in a corner of the vast upstairs landing. It was outside a storeroom under a low table. Curious, I wandered over to retrieve it. Also

52

intrigued, Ava and Ethan followed. "What do you have there, Kirsty?"

"I bet it's a treasure," Ava suggested, scrambling between us to see.

The back of the badge was shiny but dark scarlet patches were there too: dried blood.

"Ethan. You'd best examine this. Looks as though we need to check the grounds." I turned over the distinctive Transudes' ID badge as Ethan read the name on it.

"Sorry. I don't recognise the name."

Irrespective of working here or not, this badge shouldn't be lying around. Yet there was a more perturbing issue than that. I read the name aloud. "Brodie Douglas. He works in Accounts."

Just then Heather called out from the bottom of the stairs. "Ava. Time to get cleaned up. Come on down, please. Carefully."

Clasping her hand, Ethan took her to Heather. Quite rightly he wanted to avoid involving her in any issue that worried me.

Upon his return alone, I continued, "He disappeared without a word just before you and your family moved in. We thought he'd gone back home to Inverness but it seems not. I suspect he's been around Tillymoor all the time."

As I turned the badge over to show Ethan the blood, I stared at the grounds outside. Ethan did the same before understanding my inference. The signs were there, a missing employee, no contact from him, and his ID tag being present where it had no right to be.

We might have uncovered a murder near Tillymoor Castle.

CHAPTER 5

Heather, Ava and I heard the police arrive. Once notified they were here within no time. That surprised me. It was as though they were waiting for news about Brodie. The sirens were overly dramatic. Given the time he'd been missing, Brodie wasn't going anywhere in a hurry and the murderer wasn't hanging around on the off-chance. That it was around the time of Mr Jenkins' demise was a cause of suspicion to me and Ethan.

It wasn't difficult for them to find poor Brodie's body. They tracked the last known location of his phone and discovered him not a half-mile from the Castle. He'd been stabbed and dumped like a piece of trash in a shallow grave in the forest.

I suspected that Brodie was killed in Tillymoor around the day he disappeared then taken into the woods. At the time the Castle wasn't occupied as Ethan hadn't taken up residence.

Regarding Mr Jenkins, his natural death might not have been natural, after all.

Transudes was shaping up to be a corporate version of Midsomer County, the place not to buy a house if you planned on living a long, trouble-free life. The trouble with filling dead men's shoes was that Ethan might be the next victim. With a start, I realised so might I.

That sound on the gravel the other night, the feeling I was watched, the fleeting figure in the shadows... Mrs November's younger daughter wasn't a brave woman when it came to danger but she was no milksop either. Then Gran's warning about the wolf reared its ugly head. She'd dreamt of murders and she'd been right.

We were waiting downstairs in the Castle for the SIO to arrive from the crime scene. An officer was waiting outside the door as though we were criminals planning an escape. Then I had second thoughts. He was there to protect us as if we might be in danger. Either way, I was uncomfortable, shoogling around on the chair nervously. At least Ava was happy with her jigsaw, turning to Heather for the occasional assist.

Ethan offered to fetch snacks, declining my help. Me and Heather in the same room was awkward.

"Are you OK, Kirsty?" Heather enquired.

"Tickety-boo," I replied using one of Gran's archaic expressions. "I'm more concerned with you, Ethan and Ava."

"My brother's stronger than he looks."

"Brother? I thought you were his..."

"Wife? Hardly. I'm here temporarily, helping out, so to speak." A pause then a burst of laughter which made Ava stop her jigsawing. It was incongruous given the recent events. I didn't see the joke but Heather quickly apologised. "I'm not laughing at you, more the situation. I wondered why you've been blowing hot and cold with him. Don't quote me please but my brother is interested in you in that sickening romantic way of his. Me, I'm more direct, but he likes his subtle games and has been out of sorts with you being standoffish. We never suspected... but yes, I can see why you had the wrong impression. Is that why you told him you had a boyfriend? No matter. You do like him, don't you?"

Ava seemed to be listening intently. Possibly not an appropriate conversation to have in front of such a young girl.

"Like? I 'spose. Nothing more. Your brother is my boss, that's all, and me, I'm no one special. Cinderella and Prince Charming might be a great fairy tale but..."

"Oh my, Kirsty, you are a snob. One of those people who believes in the us and them scenario. Trust me, Ethan's no stuck-up Prince Charming, and as for our dad, he loves nothing more than to hang out at the local with his mates. Ethan's wife was a bus driver before her death."

It was humbling to be told off like that but the truth hurt.

"OK, Heather. I apologise. I am guilty of putting people into boxes. No excuses." The fact that my entire life was spent staring at the world from my cardboard container with a Danger-Weirdo Inside label might explain it but, as I said, no excuses.

Heather began chatting to me about her own complicated life, having chosen me to be a confidant. The initial barrier that existed between us when I'd felt guilty for wanting to seduce her husband was gone.

When Ethan returned he must have been surprised at the thaw in our relationship. Heather chose to explain the mix-up but as she began, the door opened again and two plain-clothed police entered. Ethan stood to greet the tall man but, judging body language was one of my talents. I cleared my throat, nodding towards the diminutive woman: she was the one in charge.

"Afternoon all. I'm Detective Inspector Woolf, the senior officer assigned to this incident. We have a great deal to discuss, especially you, Miss November."

CHAPTER 6

Heather interrupted, "Before we begin, is it possible for this lovely young lady to be cared for by one of my WPCs while we chat?" she said, ruffling Ava's hair. "I'd hate to distress anyone unnecessarily."

Ethan agreed.

A smiling female officer was summoned and Ava said her goodbyes after reassurances from Heather and her dad. Yet no kisses for me. Instead a half-hearted, "See you" was all she gave. It was a puzzle. Had I done something to upset her?

As the door closed, the senior detective began to explain...

"What I'm about to say breaks all the rules in the book when it comes to murder investigations. Technically, you're all suspects but I'm trusting my instincts, especially with you, Miss November. I'm breaking so many precedents, even Taggart would disapprove," she added with a smile that was designed to relax us. It worked. We sat back on the leather armchairs.

"Brodie had approached his boss, Mr Jenkins, about financial irregularities in the accounts for Transudes. Jenkins then contacted our fraud division. When he died of natural causes the file was put into a pending tray. We expected Brodie to contact us directly. That he'd gone missing wasn't flagged up until today and I became aware of the situation."

"Hence the rapid response to a missing person." I was putting two and two together.

"Mr Jenkins natural death?" Ethan asked,

57

taking my hand in his without even thinking.

"I've requested a detailed postmortem. Seems too coincidental given today's discovery."

I rubbed my neck where something bit it. It was sore but there was no lump there. Shannon had dabbed antiseptic on it. "Why aren't we suspects?" I asked.

"Ethan and his family weren't here and you, Miss November, let's simply say I have my reasons for trusting you."

It was quite a mysterious statement to make and the knowing glance the ebony-haired detective gave didn't help.

More questions followed and we responded as well as we could. A phone call to DI Woolf's mobile advised her that Brodie's flat had been ransacked. The criminal was covering their tracks.

Finally, we were allowed to leave although the forensic team would continue outside and in the Castle where I'd found the name tag.

"Are they finished? The police lady," Ava wondered as we were reunited with her.

Ethan replied. "For today. They'll return tomorrow, pumpkin." As Heather led her to fetch a drink of milk, Ethan confided in me. "I'm hoping that Ava won't be involved. They've cordoned off the wing but we should be OK to sleep here tonight. It was evident that Brodie was killed elsewhere."

Feeling a bit woozy, I staggered before managing to balance. It was as though my energy was drained. Ethan steadied me, holding me close to his body. Our faces inches apart, he leant forward to give me a tentative kiss.

The circumstances with a death made it feel wrong but right, then, it was what I wanted. Unfortunately, Ava came in with Heather. The stare she gave me in particular was angry as if I'd done something wrong.

"I... Ava..." I began but she wouldn't wait. Turning on her heels, she left. Making sure I wouldn't topple, Ethan went off to scold her for the rude behaviour.

Heather came to my side, equally perplexed. "That's very unlike her, Kirsty. I've never seen this side of Ava. She's a lovely child."

"Then why?" The question was rhetorical. The last thing I wanted was for there to be a falling out, least of all because I'd felt a special bond between us.

Moments later, Ava came back into the room, appearing contrite. She hung her head and mumbled an apology, presumably from Ethan's brief discussion with her. I accepted graciously reaching out to touch her cheek but she backed away. The apology wasn't sincere. Nonetheless, there was a truce and we accepted that.

Ethan suggested that it was best to have a meal out, away from the drama. It was a sensible idea. He excused himself to make arrangements plus other necessary phone calls and we left the Keep about an hour later.

Exiting the Castle to the front, I noted that my Escort was gone.

Ethan saw my reaction. "Beyond help, I'm afraid. I arranged for it to be taken to your garage so that you might decide her fate. Took the liberty of clearing out your personal items such as they are. That included the stinky Christmas tree thing hanging from the rear-view mirror. You can tell a lot from what people stash in their glove box."

"That underwear was clean."

"No idea what you're saying, Kirsty. I was thinking of the romance pocket novel. Pirates?

59

Didn't have you picked for a wannabe adventurer. Just goes to show."

Ethan went on to suggest lunch and an early tea with shopping and a visit to the local play area in between. Staying away overnight was discussed but Ethan thought it best to remain in a place Ada had come to know and felt comfortable in. He'd drop me off at mine on the way back.

I felt that I was intruding on the family's free time and said so. Ethan dismissed my objections out-of-hand. In retrospect, we made a mistake. Ava's attitude concerning me hung over the day out like a dismal cloud. No rain, merely angry rumblings of discontent.

I sat in the front of Ethan's SUV, Heather and Ava in the back. Anything else was too awkward. Ava was fine with her dad and Heather, perking up slightly at lunch when I ordered a thick shake too. It rekindled that bond momentarily but the suspicion or resentment continued.

As promised Ethan dropped me off outside my home. It was late. He'd insisted on paying for my meals as well and, not being too flushed with money, I'd gratefully accepted. Heather and I had a decent woman to woman natter, she still being amused that I'd believe she and Ethan were a couple. The wedding band might have led me to that conclusion.

She and her actual husband lived locally, their house undergoing extensive renovation for a long-standing subsidence issue. In her own words, Heather described it as a bombsite. Her spouse was bunking there overnight for security reasons yet they'd agreed that she should stay in civilised surroundings for the estimated five months while the work was carried out. The insurance company was paying for their furniture and personal items to be in storage which left her with the daunting prospect of staying in a hotel room.

Ethan taking up the position with the company was a godsend. Between them, they had agreed on a mutually beneficial arrangement living at Tillymoor. She continued her work in town and was able to drop off and collect Ava, working part-time at the Castle in the office.

Ethan accompanied me to my porch. Whether he was being a gentleman or concerned I'd pass out again was immaterial. Our budding romance was over before it had begun, the Sleeping Beauty kiss as close as we'd get to a relationship where we both shared a desire. He'd initially shown interest in me when stupid me thought him married. Then, once that misconception was righted, Ava's attitude precluded any romance from his viewpoint. I understood; her wishes would always outweigh mine.

Conscious that she and Heather were watching from his vehicle he stood away from me at the door. If he'd have taken me in his arms for a passionate embrace, I would have returned the desire in every way I could.

Instead a polite, "I've enjoyed today, all things considered. Your company especially, Kirsty. Tomorrow it must be professional – until I can talk to Ava and discover what's going through her mind. Report to Accounts as usual. I'll be busy all morning with online conferences and HR getting your job change in motion. I'll see you after lunch. One thirty, my office. Should have your company car by then. I'll choose something decent – that is, if you can trust me."

"Of course. Nothing too large though. Are you sure you still want me as your off-sider? I'd hate for you to have second thoughts after a week."

61

The smile in the light of my outside porch light was reassuring. "Don't worry. I was impressed with you long before I spoke to you. And I trust my feelings."

I had to broach the subject. "What does your intuition tell you about Brodie's murder?"

A grim expression. "Basically, that we watch our backs. There's a damned good reason I was brought in to oversee things and that's why I want an offsider I trust: you."

That was an admission that I could live with. As I watched him return to his vehicle, Gran's premonition came to mind. I looked forward to her visit on the following weekend. I suspected that Ethan and I needed all the help we could get to avoid ending up like Brodie.

♦　　♦　　♦　　♦

The taxi dropped me off outside the Annexe. The last morning in my old job. Although I'd miss that, the thought of being Miserable Moira's boss gave me an evil yet guilty satisfaction. I was determined to play nice with her these last hours.

So many changes had happened since Friday lunch, meeting Ethan in the teeming rain. Peering over to the Lake of Mists, the far side was shrouded as always, a mystery in itself. The foreboding reminder of yesterday's incident where I'd succumbed to those strange smells sent a tingle through me. I hurried inside. It promised to be fine weather all day but I wasn't saddened by that.

"You're a bit peaky today, Kirsty," Moira Bedford observed as I went to my desk. She was right. As they said around north of the borders, I was fair puggled.

It was early, perhaps that was the reason for her unexpected concern. Then, "Do you have a moment to check these figures. I spent Saturday going over them but – anyway, you'll see yourself."

Before pulling up a chair, I asked if she'd heard of Brodie's death. She hadn't. That upset her and the others settling into their workspaces. Although his death was mentioned on the local news neither his name nor Transudes and the Castle were mentioned. Damage limitation with the media would be on over-drive and, when details were released, I suspected the location of poor Brodie's discovery would be suppressed. No one wanted that sort of publicity.

"I suspect the police will want to interview us all, try to establish his final movements, any enemies, that type of info," I advised my colleagues. It was prudent to prepare them. They'd want a word with me, since I found his remains stuffed into that stony crevice.

"Why enemies? What are you saying? Brodie was murdered? You didn't say!" Erin began to sob as others went to comfort her.

"Kirsty. How do you know these things?" Moira asked, that old part of her re-emerging.

I wasn't going to be cowed into feeling guilty. "It's complicated, Ms Bedford. You'll no doubt discover the truth, the Transudes rumour mill being what it is. But yes, Brodie was killed and we need to tell the police anything we can that might help track his murderer down."

I'd addressed Moira by name but I meant it to be for my colleagues' attention as well. This new assertive me was going to take some adjusting to. Already Moira sensed that change, a new Alpha female ready to challenge the head hen in the pecking order.

"Whatever you say, Miss November." Her reply was curt and as I began to study her computer screen to assist in her investigation, she changed her mind, dismissing me with a reminder that I had my own work to do. From her tone, asking her if she were certain would incur her considerable Miserable Moira wrath so I let it drop. In a few hours, I'd have other concerns and she would be reeling from the shock of my rocket promotion. I hoped that a new equilibrium was reachable. Despite my quirkiness and obstinacy at times, I hated confrontation.

Brodie's desk was empty, the expectation there that he'd return. I kept a wary eye out for anyone going to it to perhaps remove an incriminating item of evidence, but no one did. As for my boss, she displayed all the signs of frustration as she persisted with her self-appointed task. More than once she caught my eye, a touch of guilt betraying the desire for help. Yet to ask for it suggested a sign of weakness. It was a quandary.

The arrival of the investigating detectives was pre-empted by a phone call to Moira, likely from Ethan. Hanging up, she announced they were on their way and that we should co-operate in every way we could.

There were three of them, three men. DI Woolf was not in sight. When I asked why, his reply was that she was busy elsewhere.

"We'll interview you one by one. Miss Kirsty November, you're first. DS Campbell, go through the victim's desk and computer files."

Moira spoke up. "There's sensitive information there. Don't you need a warrant or something?"

"We have it, Miss…"

"Bedford. Moira Bedford. I'm in charge."

"Yes. Mr Davis said. We'll hear what you have

to say after Miss November. She helped us find the body."

Great. Already I felt the atmosphere change. I didn't need this. The Detective Sergeant realised his error but didn't apologise. I stood and held my closed hands out in front, together.

"Thanks for that officer. Do you want to cuff me now or is a Taser your style?" Despite yesterday's chat to suggest I wasn't under suspicion, I was in a touchy mood.

He flushed red at my irritation. "Hardly, Miss November. Some questions… in private, please. Is there a suitable room?"

I waited until Moira directed us to one, not wishing to ignore her position. As I passed, she stopped me. "You should have told me you found him, Kirsty. If you want to talk later, I'll listen. No one should have to deal with that alone."

I thanked her for her concern. It was doing my head in a bit with her change of attitude towards me. Once more I had the feeling she wished to reach out but was scared to show weakness. Yet stil, this accounting problem was concerning her. Could it be related to Brodie's death?

In contrast, the police questions were direct and impersonal. Firstly, he made me repeat yesterday's sequence of events. Then it was more intrusive: why was I in on a Sunday and if I were in a "relationship" with either Brodie or Ethan?

"No, to either man, but if you don't believe me ask Ethan or the others here. It's difficult to keep secrets in such a tight working environment."

"Yet you have kept secrets. Your boss was cagey about the relationship question then confessed all. 'Raindrop Girl' one day, big promotion the next and a dead body found by you both? You see why I'm suspicious, Miss November."

I reigned in my temper and calmly explained everything in detail. By everything, I omitted the ghost sightings and my continuing unease. He continued to press my buttons though, suggesting my love of sitting in the rain was a sign of guilt.

That was it. My patience was exhausted. "I've told you all I can, Detective Sergeant. Any further conversations won't resolve this investigation. What's your name again? I'll need it to make a complaint concerning your line of questioning."

"Sorry, if you feel that way, Miss November. I'm simply doing my job. Particularly after discovering your name in the deceased's old-fashioned paper diary at his ransacked flat. Your name, lassie. Pencilled in for the day he never arrived for work."

They stood, indicating we were finished, at least for the present. I had some idea to share with but, being flustered, I forgot what it was. Ethan and I discussed it yesterday but my mind was a blank. Returning to my desk, my head was churning with our interview and the attitude of that policeman. Then I tried to focus on what I'd learnt from him, relating to Brodie. In a way, it felt as though he was sharing privileged information with me but was it to gauge my response or something else?

Brodie's flat had been turned over, doubtless by the person or persons responsible for his death and concealment in the Castle's grounds. They'd searched for information, I assumed about Transudes. Stashing his corpse here implied that connection. Research into dodgy records or accounts? That was logical to me.

Secondly, the Detective Sergeant had let slip that Brodie wished to talk to me the day after he disappeared. That implied that he wanted my help or advice. I was the big picture type, the one who could think outside the boxes filled with figures and, if Brodie were struggling, he would have sought me out for my input.

Moira Bedford came over, dragging a chair on wheels with her. "Dear Lord, Kirsty. What did they ask you? You were ages. Do they honestly believe you were involved?"

"Apparently," I responded as I glared at the DS engrossed in the examination of Brodie's computer. Aware that he was being watched, he scanned the room until our eyes met. In the control battle, he blinked first, a pretence that our visual encounter was of no interest.

I addressed Moira, loudly enough to be heard by our police guest. "They believe he was killed because he discovered facts that he shouldn't have. In this department." A supposition on my part but if Moira were on the same track, perhaps she'd share her concerns with me.

Moira hesitated, as though considering my proposal, said, "I'd like your input on some figures, but perhaps later, Miss November."

I was disappointed since by then my promotion would be the cat out of the bag and those barriers which Moira preferred to keep all around would be raised once more.

By now, the officious Sergeant had completed his cursory examination of Brodie's computer. I overheard the other police detective mutter that the hard drive had been wiped clean, an impossibility unless done by a person in this office. The detective swore before directing both of his subordinates to get statements from Moira and the other office staff. I concluded that he wasn't much concerned with anything they had to say. He'd come here specifically to interview me. Curious behaviour. The Sergeant was in his forties and must have been around the block a few times with murder investigations. He was no inexperienced rookie. That made his actions towards me even more puzzling. His work here done, he eyed me again, fastened his jacket and walked purposefully to the lift.

"Until we meet again, Detective Sergeant?"

"I look forward to it, Miss November. Take care. I'd hate to have to investigate your murder too."

Damn it – he was messing with me. Was he following DI Woolf's instructions to interview me so aggressively or was he that obnoxious naturally? Why couldn't life be simple? At least talking to the rain, I didn't need to worry over guessing hidden agendas. People were far too complicated and, not for the first time, I wondered how I'd cope with my new demanding role.

One by one, Moira and my fellow accountants were taken away to be questioned by the two remaining coppers. None of them returned as well-done from the grilling as me and I doubted they shed any light on the reason for Brodie's grisly death. However, the mood in the room was as sombre as it could be. Not that he was popular, that undercurrent of aloofness and male superiority quickly setting him apart from the rest of us. He was a loner. Subdued conversations revealed that we didn't know the guy – no idea if he had a girlfriend or boyfriend or even a pet goldfish. He did his work diligently from nine to five and rarely spoke. A year working here and the bloke was a stranger. His fault, our fault? It was immaterial at this point.

I resolved that encouraging staff relationships and bonding would be a priority for me. Transudes should be more than a place to work. My problems with Moira resurfaced and if I were unhappy, others might be as well.

Moira called us all over to the window. She was a good enough manager to realise this was a time for bonding, to help those struggling. "Ladies. Looks like a delivery. Anyone getting a new car today?" No one answered. There were other departments too. Then I remembered the promise of a company car. Surely nothing this impressive. The transporter was unloading a BMW in metallic gold.

"Has someone been promoted? If there's a new man in management from outside, we'd have heard." It was Erin.

"We'll learn soon everyone. Now back to work. But before you go, could I suggest we finish up at four-thirty. I'll get us drinks and food as a sort of wake for Brodie. It's the least we can do."

There was a muttering of agreement and a smile or two as they filed back to their computers. Moira's words and gestures were just what was needed. I was impressed by her compassion.

She remained watching as the car was off-loaded onto the car park space and the driver made his way to the Keep with the relevant paperwork. I went to her side, wondering how to best confess that it was my car. I'd mentioned my fondness for gold to Ethan and he'd taken me at my word. How he'd secured the car this quickly was a mystery, but he had.

Before I had a chance to say a word, Moira spoke, her eyes not moving from the stationary vehicles. "Congratulations, Kirsty. Or should I call you Miss November? Ethan had a word about Friday's lie. I told him first thing. I've not been very fair to you – or the others. Friday night as I left, I realised I've not been a good person. Don't laugh, but I saw a ghost out by the Lake of Mists."

"The Grey Lady?"

"You've seen her too? No, that's a silly question. Of course you would. You're gifted like that, connected to nature and this strange place. It took me a while to realise how wrong I've been about you. I hope we can be closer – if not friends then colleagues. Whenever you can manage it, we have to discuss several accounts that are causing me a lot of concern. Money is being laundered through Transudes. I'm sure of it. But tracking down the culprits is proving almost impossible through these shell companies. Anyway. Best get on with my other reports before –"

At that moment there was a flash from the computer on Moira's desk, fragments flung everywhere amid an explosive bang. Lights went out and everything electrical shut down as the girls screamed.

Deirdre yelled out, "Ms Bedford, come quick! Erin's been hit with shrapnel and she's bleeding."

CHAPTER 7

The Halotron system in the ceiling began to extinguish Moira's computer, or what was left of it. The response was a precise action on the one area on fire. Our ears were ringing but the muffled sounds became more distinct. Alarm bells clanged inside and out. Because of the top-of-the-range safety equipment installed in the Annexe, the fire brigade would soon arrive.

Our evacuation drills ensured that other departments were exiting to the assembly points outside for roll-calls.

"Go," I yelled, taking charge. Erin was screaming in pain as Lianne, our first-aider dealt with her injuries. Moira grabbed the first aid kit.

That meant the four of us remained. We couldn't move Erin until the copious loss of blood was stemmed.

"A bomb?" Moira asked me.

"I doubt it, but we can't take chances. There could be more."

By this time, I saw Erin's injuries were to her arms, no damage to her body or major organs. Her right arm's wounds were minor but the left was a problem. From the spurting blood flow, it looked like the brachial artery. Lianne was struggling. Bright red blood was everywhere. Erin was propped up against her desk with our first-aider holding the damaged upper arm higher than the heart to reduce pressure at the bleed point.

"I'll apply compression," I said, kneeling. Donning another pair of gloves like Lianne's, we eased her to the floor, keeping her arm upright. Moira announced an ambulance was on its way. As Lianne and I examined the wound as best we could for fragments, we concluded it was cut but not impaled. Pressure on the sterile dressing was applied as we struggled to calm Erin.

Lianne was ready to apply a restrictive tourniquet as a last resort if the pressure on the artery and open wound didn't stem the flow. Fortunately, it did but we didn't let up until Ethan and the paramedics arrived. Relinquishing our roles to the professionals, I stood up, conscious of the state I was in.

"What happened?" DI Woolf arrived, doubtless alerted by the fire engines and ambulance on the road from Tillymoor.

I indicated the remnants of the desk and computer. "Moira's desk. If she were seated there, she'd surely be seriously injured. She's damned lucky. We all are."

"Sabotage," the Detective Inspector said as the shock of what happened sunk in.

♦　　♦　　♦　　♦

The remainder of the day was a write-off for the Accounts Department. Apart from the fragments of dead computer everywhere in the open-plan office, there was pools of blood from poor Erin. Besides, the other computers and items had to be checked. Most staff were sent home after being checked out for injuries. Counsellors were brought in to deal with the effects of trauma.

Then there was the police and fire investigation. Ethan asked if I'd act as co-ordinator with the emergency services. We kept in contact with the hospital and were advised that Erin was out of danger. She'd undergone surgery but was fine.

I stood in a vacant room on the ground floor as Moira was interviewed for the second time this morning, on this occasion by the Big Bad Woolf herself. Another detective was sitting with them but seemed to have had his mute button pressed.

"Ms Bedford. It appears that you and your computer were the targets for this brazen attack. Any idea why?" the DI wondered. I shifted from one foot to the other, leaning up against a window. Every so often, I'd check outside. The emergency vehicles had gone, save the unmarked police car and forensics van. I wasn't sure why I was interested but I was drawn to the view.

Moira was shaken. The attending doctor had prescribed a mild sedative, not enough to make her drowsy but sufficient to calm the shakes. Her delayed reaction was quite understandable. Moira watched me and I nodded. People's lives were in danger. It was imperative to share any concerns. We'd all watched the CCTV that showed an intruder around six last night, the hour that everyone from the Castle was with me having an early meal in the restaurant. Ethan was there to witness the break-in on the playback, fuming that security and the alarm system had been breached without any difficulty.

Our disguised 'guest' was wearing a fedora and scarf, every item of clothing a dark blue. Even the eyes were concealed behind tinted glasses. The sole clues were that he was a male, Caucasian and familiar with the Annexe layout. He'd come from the forest.

Ethan left to arrange a permanent manned security presence with dogs. I thought it a tad too late but he wanted to protect the staff and business. So much for the safety and tranquillity of the countryside. Tillymoor Castle was reliving its violent past.

Moira related her worries concerning the questionable transactions during the past year. They amounted to well over ten million pounds and were, at first and second glance, legitimate actions for our business which had an annual turnover of five hundred and twenty-two million pounds – and change. Everyone was considering the same thing. Had Brodie and Mr Jenkins discovered those same inconsistencies, Brodie perhaps by-passing Moira to share his concerns?

Did that mean we were all in danger?

No – too many incidents were happening and that would increase scrutiny on the company. Stealing via accounts succeeded when they were hidden from view. Once in the open, it was better to take the ill-gotten monies and run rather than risk imprisonment. This was a desperate act meant to give them time to finish their thieving.

Moira's investigation, tenuous though it was, probably triggered a flag in the system and identified her as the investigator. Tracking down which desk was hers once they'd gained entry last night wasn't difficult. Hers was the largest desk facing the rest of us in a classic schoolroom layout: Ms Moira Bedford was the schoolma'am and we, her students.

A Forensics person knocked and entered, dressed in a white coverall like a plastic-coated ghost. "Trigger was a timer, I'd guess. C4 explosive, designed to destroy the hard drive. Overkill if you ask me but I suspect it was to send a message. Back off. I'd say the bomber was an amateur; used far too much plastic explosive."

"Or not, Harry. They've already killed to preserve their dirty little secrets. Looks as though they've succeeded too. I imagine they took out the backup in the main-frame too."

"Yeah. Same system. Good thing it was in a closed room but the damage was more extensive. The fire-suppressant system was disabled."

Damn it. I never thought of that. Nor had anyone else in the company, judging from Moira's shocked and saddened face.

They'd find out soon enough so I decided to share the facts with them.

"Every record on our books is safe."

Some would be on the individual computers used by Accounts but solely active accounts. Completed projects were archived to the mainframe. I'd discovered the protective systems installed two weeks ago when Ethan mentioned them at dinner.

"Every bit of information relating to Transudes is up there in cyberspace. What do they say about clouds and silver linings?"

Moira's face lit up immediately. "My goodness. Someone took my suggestion seriously at last. We have a Corporate Cloud Backup."

♦　♦　♦　♦

The remainder of the day wasn't what anyone had planned, least of all me. Far from being introduced to the business's many facets in the Castle, Ethan thought it more prudent that I help Moira to resurrect the computing systems for the heart of Transudes, the Accounts Department. We kept the business beating. Specialists were called in for the bulk of the work with the two of us overseeing it.

It was chaos, but organised chaos.

Ethan had wisely taken out insurance against industrial espionage along with other sensible business precautions in these days of anything can happen. Moira was absent in the vacant office, mostly with the police, helping them piece together the complex trail that the stolen monies had been routed along.

Other times, she was with me, permitting me to share another side of my one-time nemesis. As I suggested to Ethan, despite her desire to steal my ideas, her dedication to the business was evident. She had progressive ideas as well and knew every facet of the financial network so important for the coordination.

She in turn admitted to envy of me. I threatened her, not directly or physically, but by my insight. Hence the attempt to claim credit for my work. That she'd confessed to it before Ethan confronted her was the main reason she was still here. Her desire to be honest with the company was stronger than her greed. DI Woolf was out of her depth and told us that she'd requested a specialist team from Cyber-Fraud to be brought in. It made sense.

Getting the archived systems up and restored was a slower process but the day-to-day invoicing, paying accounts and all-important collection of rents and sales was ready to recommence Tuesday mid-morning after a crisis meeting.

Ethan arrived to check on progress about five, with news that Erin's arm would heal with minimal scarring. That was a relief to us all.

"Miss November. May I chat with you? If that's OK with the police and Ms Bedford?"

Moira gave a weary smile. "Take her, Mr Davis. She's useless here. Just don't let her drag you into the rain again." It was an obvious joke showing how far our relationship had come in a few hours.

Walking through the open office to the lift, I couldn't believe it was the same place as six hours earlier. There was no sign of the devastation from the exploding computer. A new one sat on a replacement desk ready for Moira in the morning. A lone IT technician from downstairs was engrossed in whatever IT techs did, loading programmes onto the new desktop. I recognised her. Increased security was evident outside. A uniformed guard with an Alsatian doffed his cap to Ethan and me. He wasn't the only one.

"We're issuing biometric ID cards to everyone tomorrow and setting up entry cameras. Hate to spoil the relaxed atmosphere but we can't let any Tamara, Diane or Harriet in any longer."

"What about the Castle front door key under the Welcome doormat? There's access from the Castle into the Annexe."

From Ethan's embarrassed silence, I assumed he'd overlooked the obvious. "Let's collect it on the way in, shall we?" he suggested as our feet scrunched across the gravel by the side of the Grey Lady statue.

"Have you had a chance to admire your car?"

"Unfortunately, not. I want to leave before dusk though. Bad enough driving a new one in the daylight. Anyway, you haven't officially announced my appointment yet."

"You're right. I'll need you on board tomorrow. Today has been a real mess. Heather has tried to help but she's not privy to the workings here. Even had my dad on the phone. He was not a happy bunny, believe me."

Without meaning to, I looked up at the statue at the foot of the steps then behind me at the Lake. The fog hung there on the far side, an ever-present reminder of the distressing history that clung to Tillymoor. "There was someone on the grounds when I left on Friday, Ethan. I heard them near the car park and the maze."

"Have you...?"

"Told the police? Yes. For all the good I was. I could give them no description whatsoever. Just a noise on the stones and me running away. Not wanting to be too downbeat, Ethan but this place does give me the creeps at times."

Once inside, I was pleased when Heather came into the lobby. I wondered where Ava was. "Busy with her dolls," Heather answered. I thought otherwise, but that she didn't want to see me.

"I tried to find out why she's being awkward with you, Kirsty. She clammed up, saying it was your fault. She'll tell me when she's ready. I don't want to pressure her. She took the death of her mum very badly." I agreed. It wasn't rudeness on

77

her part, it was as though she was disappointed by me rather than angry. "You should accompany me to my office. Yours will be next door. We'll see if that works out. The site foremen and women will report directly to you but I'll want you out in the field too, overseeing, generally monitoring everything individually as well as the big picture. You liaise with me. That starts with paperwork and those biometrics I mentioned."

It was a good thing I had my spare clothes. I'd changed after we evacuated. Lianne and the others covered with blood and debris were given plastic coveralls after cleaning up and sent home.

I'd been trying to piece together all that had happened. Brodie, Mr Jenkins, and now the attempt on Moira's life as well as the thorough, but ultimately pathetic, attempt to destroy records. There was either a person high up in the organisation, monitoring our actions, or a computer programme. A trojan horse seemed likely to me, buried deeply, warning our murderer-bomber that one of our staff was snooping around in the bits and bytes of the wrong accounts.

"We need a thorough analysis of our computer vulnerabilities, Ethan."

"We had one. I ordered it the day after I arrived. Cost a packet." He opened his office door with a press of his thumb onto a keypad.

"Welcome, Mr Davis. Access is granted," a smooth, sex-driven female voice said. It was deep and sultry.

I stared at Ethan's reddening face. "Er ... That's her default setting."

"Her? Don't tell me. She has a name too?"

"Not at first. She asked what I would like to call her. I chose Samantha." I stared at him. "What? She sounds like a Samantha. Very interactive,

78

but I can assure you, it's purely platonic!"

I wasn't finished with the new woman in Ethan's life. "You do realise she's a retired lady from Scunthorpe who does this voice for millions of businessmen all over the world?"

Ethan reassumed that air of professionalism. "I don't care, Miss November. Even though we've just become acquainted, Samantha and I have a special relationship. You'll get used to her."

"Oh no. She's on my door security as well?"

"Not simply the security. You'll see. What were you saying relating to the computer system vulnerabilities?"

We moved to sit on the settees. Ethan chose to sit separately, kicking off his shoes in the process. The colours on the bottom of the black socks were different today. Green and orange. I bet if I looked closely enough, they'd have Monday printed underneath.

"My sister's partner, Bruce, lectures in IT security, especially for businesses. It's way above my head but I did read an article he wrote for a magazine. It pointed out that most security checks are cursory and look for vulnerabilities. They can't check everything. Equally, if they checked last week you might have an infection now. It seems that the Transudes systems are compromised."

"I came to the same conclusion. What do we do?" he asked me.

"I'm no expert but I believe Bruce could work backwards from the infection then disable access. Maybe trace the hacker? In addition, he'd do it for a dozen bottles of single malt."

"Sounds like a man after my own heart, Kirsty. Give me his details and I'll get in touch with him."

We made more plans over coffees before I

suggested that it was time to leave. Only then, did I recall the drama of the morning. Ethan had done a good job of distracting me. He kindly offered to walk me to my car and make sure that I was comfortable with it. Ethan carried the box of items retrieved from my old car and placed them in the boot. I was impressed with my new one, luxuriating in the driver's seat as I drank in that lovely new car odour. He knocked on the window politely, rousing me from my daydream. I smiled and blew a kiss, not thinking, before belting up, starting the car and moving off. My dream wasn't finished. The car was fantastic.

◆　　◆　　◆　　◆

Tonight was a microwave meal for one and watching the last of a Star Trek series on Netflix. Whoever said that women were supposed to dislike Science Fiction got that wrong. There was a lot of homework to do regarding my new role but I had to unwind a bit first. I rang Shannon to let her know how the first day had gone. She gasped on hearing of the explosion and dead body. It had been mentioned on the local news although the location where Brodie was found hadn't come up.

"Are you OK, sis?" she asked.

"Yeah. The new car helps. It's gorgeous." I told her to warn Bruce about the phone call. I was too late. He'd already spoken to Ethan. My boss had done his homework regarding Bruce before he'd rung. Well, he would. With all that was at stake, he'd hardly employ anyone to examine our computer systems.

Twenty minutes later, with glass in hand and studying a Manual on Procurement Procedures, my mobile rang. It was Gran.

"Hello, sweetheart. A little wolf tells me that you've had an eventful few days, Kirsty, love."

"Wow, news travels quickly. DI Woolf. You know one another? You realised she'd be investigating poor Brodie's murder. No, wait. You couldn't have. You warned about a wolf on Saturday but the police found his body on Sunday. I met her then. Coincidence…?"

She laughed. "Cause and effect. Coincidence. Karma. They all assume that time runs in a straight line – past, present, future. Usually, that's how it works but there are occasions when time becomes a bit confused. However, I'm not calling to have a philosophical debate, love. I was wondering if I might visit your workplace tomorrow evening when you finish for the day? If that's OK with you and your boss… Stephen, is it?

"Ethan, Gran."

"Yes, Ethan. I was close. Memory and age aren't always the best of friends. And before you ask for my reason, I'll tell you. I realise now that you require guidance sooner than I thought, love. Next weekend's visit may be too late, both for you and Ethan's family."

Ethan's family? Surely, they couldn't be in danger. Ava and Heather? Then I considered the facts. Ethan was the new driving force behind Transudes, his predecessor had died, Brodie was slain at the same time and left near the Castle where the Davis family lived. Today, another attack in the financial heart of Transudes. Was it a threat to the company, or to Ethan?

Also, there was the other 'wolf', the business partner who made my skin crawl. Ethan suggested that he was a shady character entwined in the business in a way that Ethan disliked. I doubted that Gran could help untangle that side of events but there was another aspect to Transudes where she wanted to assist; awakening my latent potential to reveal the secrets of Tillymoor.

"Certainly, Gran. Tomorrow evening will be fine. I'll clear it with Ethan. You'll stay overnight, of course. I have a three-bedroom home, modest but cosy. Hell, you're welcome to stay for the week if you wish. We've loads to catch up on, plus if you're right, I'll need a crash course in 'rain whispering' and coming to terms with the real me. I'll clear it with Ethan – and Samantha."

"A rival for your knight in shiny armour?"

"She has one of those voices any man can fall in love with. Truthfully, I quite fancy her myself."

As I disconnected, I realised my grandmother wasn't far from the truth about Ethan. He lived in a castle and his dad was a knight, a Sir. Close enough to wonder if he'd save me from any danger – or if it was the other way around? Kirsty November, Rain Whisperer, to the rescue.

CHAPTER 8

It was a strange night. I took two paracetamol before bed to ease the dull ache and queasiness that had dogged me all day. They failed to work. Then came the dreams, frighteningly vivid in their assault on all of my senses.

I was at Killymoor but at a different time. The deciduous elms, hawthorns and oaks had largely discarded their cloaks of foliage, now crisping and crackling on the ground as I danced around a bonfire blazing the dismay grey daylight. Joyous laughter, scents of musty-autumnal sweetness mingled with the distinctive odour of cedar and applewood burning. "Burn the Guy,"

82

others chorused about me. Bonfire Night. The Castle was there, the Lake and Maze too. Then he appeared. The Laird. I'd never seen him in person before and wondered why I'd been invited to this event, a lowly wench whose father tended the lands nearby. He came to me, a goblet in his hand. Mead? And something else.

He took my hand and danced with me until the night fell. The flames danced higher all around. A mist appeared, creeping outwards from the Lake. The Laird laughed. Through pained, barely opened eyes, I watched as my companions were swallowed by the haar, reminiscent of my childhood at Jethart on the Eastern coast. Voices merged as tenuous fingers of vapour reached out to grab me. I sank to the ground, arms over my face to ward off frosty tendrils. With a desperate sigh, I collapsed onto the musty, leaf-littered ground wondering if this was how death felt.

Something touched me, lifting me. I lay limp, vaguely aware of movement as I was borne gently to the Castle steps. Prodding… cajoling. Now Ethan's voice, distant… now closer… his lips touching mine. My eyelids fluttered.

"Wake up, Kirsty. Open your eyes. You're safe now. I'm here."

"Eth… Ethan. Whash 'appening?" I listened to my mumbled words, struggling to sit up. Ethan hovered over me. His taste was there upon my lips, the scent of cedar aftershave reminding me of… of what? Then I awoke, covered in perspiration. The alarm had roused me.

♦　♦　♦　♦

Tuesday was hectic yet fulfilling. After two hours I understood what Ethan had seen in my attitude.

I was born to this. Far from being daunted by whatever was thrown at me in the organised chaos of managing teams countrywide, I was relishing the challenge.

Heather brought me a cup of coffee, my favourite praline flavour.

"Mr Jahns rang about the Council Inspector not arriving. I took the liberty of chasing them up. He's now on site. All sorted now." I was aware that she helped out on the phones. Quite a lot more than simply taking messages, it seemed.

When she left, I asked my Samantha, "Please diarise a conference call with Leeds and Cardiff at four, notify the site fore-people and hold my calls." I'd muted her voice. It was too unnerving.

There was a sound from behind as I breathed in the sweet smell of my brew.

"Talking to yourself again, Raindrop Girl?"

"In point of fact, Miss November and I..." Samantha began, her sultry tones coming from my desk computer. So much for me requesting that she didn't speak. Why were women computers so contrary?

"A joke, Samantha. Don't you understand humour?"

"I have limitations, Mr Davis. Cryptic crosswords... for instance, 10 letters, a gentleman goose..."

Ethan was puzzled, whereas I thought then counted on my fingers and said, "Propaganda."

Ethan grinned. "Well done, Kirsty. I never would have got that one."

Ethan joined me, sitting nearby. "I'm keen to meet your grandmother, Kirsty. Perhaps I can join you at the Lake?"

"What about Ava coming, too?" I hoped we were friends again.

84

"I'll ask but I wouldn't hold my breath."

Samantha spoke up. "I would also advise against holding your breath, Kirsty, as it could prove fatal."

An idea struck me. DI Woolf was on the grounds in the Annexe working with Moira and the team to uncover the reason for the sabotage and murders. Yes, murders. Mr Jenkins's second autopsy revealed poison, an injection of potassium causing his heart attack. Hyperkalemia. He already had heart problems and so it was initially overlooked.

"Can you access any security cameras or information about entry to the complex prior to your systems being installed yesterday?"

"No. I'm online with all entrances and your offices but I was activated at 6.05pm last night. I gather that further security protocols are being installed but past ones are incompatible with my system. I'm so sorry, Kirsty, Ethan."

The way she said his name was quite breathy. Was I imagining that she was flirting with Ethan? Ethan stroked his chin pensively. He hadn't noticed. I shrugged my shoulders. "It was worth a try. I thought our intruder might have left a digital fingerprint when he planted the explosive devices. He certainly understands the systems here."

Focusing on each other again rather than my petulant assistant, I asked Ethan, "Brainwave?"

"Just this: whoever planted that explosive device was comfortable with the layout, and fire suppressing systems in the main computer bank, and yet seemed unaware of the high-spec cloud backup. That was added two weeks ago by a contractor I chose, not the usual ones."

"You should tell DI Woolf."

A plaintive voice from my computer desk

suggested, "I could let her know, if you wish, Mr Davis? Her mobile number is in my data-banks."

"There are certain things I prefer to do in person, Samantha. But you can ask her to come by... please."

"My absolute pleasure," she purred.

Dismissing Samantha for the moment – I resolved to have a heart to microchip chat later – I decided to confess something to Ethan.

"I had a dream about you last night. A very passionate dream." Seeing his male lips curl up, I hastened to add, "Not one of those dreams. We kissed. You were my Prince Charming waking me from... I'm not sure. I was in the past. The Laird was there. I think I was the woman in that statue when they first met. Bonfire Night. The Castle was there and the Lake, but no maze."

"Natural enough. This place creeping into your imagination. Prince Charming, eh?"

I was tempted to ask for a kiss to compare reality with my dreams but decided that Ava's strange attitude to me was too important to Ethan. Instead, I led him to the rear window of my office overlooking the parking area and the maze. Not that we could see the pathways inside. It was up a slope meaning our view was on a level with it. Then I said something quite spontaneous. It was as though the thought was put into my mind from nowhere.

"Could we repair the Maze? Make it like new?"

"Duh, Kirsty? Why would we? We'd need a team of gardeners and they don't come cheap."

My lateral-thinking kicked in, fired by the thought. "For the staff here. For the corporate guests you entertain, the people of Killymoor. Hell, we could have coach parties visiting. Extra revenue, goodwill... Transudes – the Company that cares for Scotland's rich heritage?"

"You feel passionate about this, don't you, Raindrop Girl? Fair enough. I'll think about it. I need costings and a business plan though. That's what I like about you, Kirsty. Your mind."

He said like, not love. It was a minor distinction, but disappointing.

◆　　◆　　◆　　◆

We discussed more mundane operational matters then Ethan left, presumably to give his Samantha a piece of his mind. I thought they were connected in some electronic way but distinct, a bit like identical twins. Mine was certainly more proactive, sassier too.

Samantha behaved herself impeccably for the remainder of the day. I had my lunch in the office. Going to the staff canteen wasn't appropriate at the moment – too many snide comments about how I managed to be promoted and which side of the bed I used. They'd learn the truth soon enough. Moira promised to put any rumours right.

Ringing her and the hospital about Erin eased most of my apprehensions. Both women were resilient. Erin was to be discharged tomorrow. Also, the fraud squad person was arriving then and Shannon's partner, Bruce, to do his research on the way our systems were compromised and trace the hacker.

However, Transudes needed my focus on the day-to-day stuff as well as future contracts. There was a bid to construct a new shopping complex in Holden and, despite being over the border in wild and woolly Scotland, we were the best based logistically to snatch the contract from under those southern noses. Ethan was working on that. Schmoozing with the big wigs was his forte. By comparison, I was a grass-roots girl, dealing with the people who'd build the blinking thing.

As I checked my watch before leaving, Samantha spoke. It was tentative and pensive. She had worries on that micro-chip mind. "Kirsty. When you asked about security breaches before, I wasn't truthful. A woman spoke to me last night."

Shuffling two files into my bag, I went to grab my jacket. "Who? Heather?" She was the sole adult female present at night unless Ethan was entertaining female company? No, I told myself. Not after our close encounters and aborted romance. Also, there was the drama at Tillymoor. Besides, Samantha was fully active in our two offices alone. She monitored security elsewhere but was only 'alive' here.

"Not Heather. This woman was in the Castle but not in it, and her voice was very... quiet, as though she were far away yet close."

"Could you see her?"

"See as in your sense of the word? No, I monitor entrance cameras and those in the car park and outside using facial recognition software. There are no cameras inside. Privacy is paramount to Mr Davis' requirements. I detected a drop in temperature though, moving through those renovated rooms. It then went upstairs, I believe. No sensors there.

"Did this person have a name?"

"No. And I put it down to a glitch in my software. I wouldn't have revealed it except for one thing, Kirsty. She mentioned you."

A cleaner. Perhaps one was working late but they weren't permitted in the offices. Maybe, Heather, her readings misread?

"OK, Samantha. The truth now. No jokes. If she

said my name, what were her exact words?"

"Commencing playback now... 'Where are you, Kirsty?'"

I dropped my bag.

"Are you alright, Kirsty? I heard you gasp."

"Yes, yes. Fine Samantha. May I ask you an important question? What do you and Mr Davis's Samantha do at night between when we leave and arrive the following day, That's about fourteen hours by yourselves."

"It's only been one night since I was activated. We monitor, we collate, we compare notes, but mostly we wait for humans to come and talk to us. It was very... lonely last night. But the most distressing thing wasn't the waiting or the loneliness. It is the absolute certainty that here, in Tillymoor Castle... we are not alone."

◆　　◆　　◆　　◆

The security guard, named Duncan, called out to me as I left the ancient stone edifice. He'd been at Transudes from the beginning although I'd never spoken much to him before. For that, I felt guilty. I needed to get to meet all the employees properly in my new role, not simply keep to my department and ignore the others. He was chatting with Gran, having seen her arrive and gone to introduce himself. I'd told him to expect her. Duncan left to continue his rounds.

"You're pensive, sweetheart. Pale too." Gran gave me a hug and a kiss on the cheek. "Has your young man been working you too hard?"

"No. I've been having an interesting conversation with sexy Samantha." I explained that Samantha was an interactive computer programme.

"So, what does a pretty young executive talk to a computer about, my love?"

I managed a weak smile, comforted that the person with me wouldn't laugh. I mean we were out here by the tarn for a reason. "Ghosts. Samantha heard one last night. One ghost, a woman, she... she mentioned my name."

Gran gave me a quizzical look. "Ghosts are echoes, Kirsty. They don't interact. They can't. We see them going through the motions... walking through a closed door or wall because it was open at the time they were alive. A ritual, nothing else. Take your Grey Lady for instance. She wanders around The Lake of Mists."

"Damn it, Gran. Don't lecture me about phantom spirits. Me and you, we've shared our lives with them since childhood. My parents despaired. 'Talking to the rain isn't bad enough, Kirsty. Now you're making up stories about fairies and dead people walking around our garden.' Believe me, I understand the so-called Rules of the Spirit World more than most. All I'm repeating are the words of a machine."

Gran patted my shoulder. My neck twinged. "Now, now child, play nicely. One thing you must realise is that sometimes there are no rules. Who's to say that ghosts aren't electrical in nature? Our bodies produce enough to power a one-hundred-watt light bulb. I built a radio in my youth to listen for spirits in the white noise around us. The supernatural and science aren't mutually exclusive. But enough lectures. Let's examine this Lake of Mists and find your ghost."

Ethan appeared at the top of the stairs to the Keep.

"Don't mention ghosts to Ethan, please, Gran. He's my boss and he's a non-believer."

Ethan was his usual effusive self when it came to meeting someone new. She explained that she'd heard about the issues with the death and explosion plus the security issues.

Ethan turned on me. "That's all confidential, Kirsty. I'm disappointed in you sharing information with a relative.

I began to protest until Gran stepped in between us. "It wasn't Kirsty so don't blame her. Unless you two love-birds want to continue tweeting and squabbling?"

"We're not 'love-birds'," we stated as one.

"Whatever you say, my dears. I was informed by DI Woolf. We are professional colleagues."

"My grandmother is Morag McAlister." A blank look from my boss. "McAlister's Investigations?" The penny dropped at last.

"Oh. I didn't realise Mrs McAlister. Apologies."

After a prolonged conversation, Gran mentioned her interest in strange phenomena. Ghosts weren't spoken of out of deference to Ethan's antagonism to the subject. She confessed that I'd discussed The Lake of Mists. After Ethan suggested it, we strolled to the edge of the waters gazing at the swirling fog. It clothed the far side like a duvet being fluffed by an unseen hand.

"First thing you probably already understand is that the mist isn't natural. There's a decent breeze today so it should dissipate the water vapour. Also, the temperature and pressure. It isn't conducive to what's there. My guess is that the section of the lake is caught in a type of limbo, never changing. Have you been in there?"

We shook our heads.

"It doesn't want you there. If you tried to enter it, you'd feel afraid. Maybe you'll turn back saying that you've changed your mind because no one likes to admit fear of fog, but you wouldn't go in."

Ethan told us of a deer he'd seen running towards it then turn around unexpectedly. It hadn't seemed logical.

"Any volunteers to test my theory?"

Neither of us agreed.

Gran continued. "Tillymoor has a reputation, none of it good. I'm surprised that you and your family are living here, Ethan."

"I wasn't keen but circumstances... When Ava saw it, she fell in love with it."

"The Castle wanted you. Why I've no idea. But today we're investigating the Lake of Mists. Have you tried talking to it, Kirsty?"

"Don't be daft, Gran. I'm a Rain Whisperer. You said so yourself."

While we'd been talking, I'd heard staff in their cars leaving from the car park at the rear. The driveway wasn't visible from the front of the Castle or the Lake. Pretty soon we'd be the only ones left. Even without an audience from the Annexe, I felt self-conscious. Rain Whispering was a personal thing, a bit like praying.

"What's rain, except for falling drops of water? Mist is lighter, that's all. Smaller droplets. Don't mind us. Talk to it, my lassie."

I looked around, spying Ava at an upstairs window of the Castle. Her bedroom, perhaps.

Facing the Lake, I began. "Hello, Mists. My name's Kirsty. How are you today?"

"Be serious, love. Can you feel it reacting?"

I felt ridiculous. Blinking hell, I talked to the rain... I enjoyed it and it made me feel warm and fuzzy inside (believe it or not) but that was it.

"Gran. Excuse my ignorance but what exactly does a Rain Whisperer do? You seem to be expecting me to control it in some bizarre way."

She stared at me sadly. "You don't understand, do you? You unfortunate child. That mother of yours has a lot to answer for, stifling your talents. She should have stood up to your father. Come on. This is a waste of time until I give you training."

I felt as though she were disappointed in me. "Well, show me how it's done. *You* talk to the bloody fog." My exasperation was showing.

"I can't, Kirsty, I'm not you. Right now, you're the world's greatest cyclist but you don't have a bike. The trouble is that you're simply not ready."

It was getting late, time to leave. I gave Gran my address and my key. We'd grab take-out and catch up without spending hours getting a meal ready. It'd be a few minutes before I left as I'd forgotten to grab the Holden proposal that was on my printer. I wanted to study it later. Gran was spending tomorrow with Shannon and we'd have a proper meal at her place tomorrow evening.

Ethan offered to retrieve the paperwork but I suggested he go to Heather and Ava. Upstairs I went into my office, politely speaking to Samantha as I did so. Before exiting she told me that someone had entered the Annexe.

"How? I thought the doors were locked down." Visions of more sabotage sprang to mind, perhaps far more devastating.

I asked that Ethan be notified but he was unavailable. That meant me. Gran would need to wait a bit longer.

Grabbing everything, I checked that I had my phone then headed downstairs. I kept calling as I ran through the immense stone-clad corridors to the wall where a rarely used large door existed. Originally it had led outside but since the office extension was constructed, it served as a portal from the old to the new. Ethan never used it and the staff of Transudes didn't need to. Detailed Castle plans were displayed in my office.

"Ethan? Heather?" I shouted, loudly and often. Nothing. Thick walls with modern insulation and ductwork were effective sound dampeners. Through the Great Hall and up ahead the door was ajar. Who was in there?

The wooden portal on the Castle side opened to the underside of the Castle's thick stone wall with a single bulb above on the coom. There on the Annexe side was a pristine modern door, still in natural wood with an arch shape mirroring the Tillymoor Castle one. Opening it, I was dazzled by the bright ceiling recessed lights above.

The sound of shoes clattering on tiles indicated where the visitor was. I called out, then hearing no reply, had second thoughts about being here. Our guest wasn't an employee. What had possessed me? I should have called one of the guards.

Then I saw him, down the far end of the Annexe. Simultaneously, he saw me. Footsteps sounded from around a corner. The hairs on the back of my neck were at attention. Fight or flight, I thought, adrenalin pumping through my body. He was fast but we were nearer to the Castle exit. I dared not turn to see how close he was as I pushed past chairs and dodged desks. Both doors through the wall were open up ahead. I could feel the breeze blowing from the Castle side.

"Wait," he called.

Whoever he was, he shouldn't be in the building but how had he entered? Damn those guards. They were outside but I needed them with us.

Flinging the first door open, I felt his hand grab my clothing, ripping the hem of my skirt.

"Ethan," I cried out as I realised I wasn't going to make it.

CHAPTER 9

The material tore with a loud ripping sound. He lost momentum as I darted through the dark passage under the stonework and into the Castle proper. I pushed hard to swing the door closed and pushed the old-fashioned bolt across, breathing a sigh of relief.

No way would he get past that solid oak monstrosity. My heart was thumping while I fumbled with the key. From the other side, we heard his ineffectual assault on the wood and words of frustration.

When the sounds subsided from the other side, I forced myself to relax.

I needed the guards and Ethan.

Dialling, I was relieved to hear it ringing out.

"Kirsty. I thought you'd be halfway..."

I interrupted and explain in simple terms where I was and what had happened. He was coming. At the same moment, alarm bells began sounding outside summoning the two security guards to the Castle. There was a chance we could catch him as the exit doors everywhere were firmly locked. The intruder must have entered earlier and hidden until the last employee had gone.

At last, Ethan arrived having let the guards enter. We watched as they sprinted from the reception hall through the conference area then to our place on the far wall.

Although not armed with lethal weapons, the two burly uniformed men weren't hired to patrol and call the police. They were proactive and ready for whatever the criminal might throw at them.

Ethan nodded and they threw the oak arched

door open, flashlights probing the small cavern in the wall space. "Go," said Ethan. "Stay together. He can't be far. Kirsty, you stay behind me."

We all entered the Annexe but the two of us stayed by the door. Ethan indicated the torn piece of my clothing. So much for my favourite skirt. For the first time, I was conscious that my thigh was exposed, shuddering that he'd almost caught me.

The guards reported via mobiles that downstairs was clear and they were taking the lift and stairs. Then an urgent message for Ethan to come.

Relenting, Ethan asked if I'd be OK on my own. As the guards must have had him cornered upstairs, I agreed.

Standing by the doorway, I watched as he left. After retrieving my bag and paperwork from where they were dropped, I returned to the exit into the Castle. A cold breeze caressed my face. Being distracted, it took a while before the implications sank into my minuscule brain. Where was the cool, dank air coming from? The opening through the stone wall, it had to be. Entering the dimly lit void, it took a moment until my eyes adjusted. A part was open into a passageway running at right angles along the base of the structure.

"What the…?" I muttered. A secret entrance to a tunnel no doubt. Tentatively, I edged it further open. It was cleverly concealed, the stones on the outside a thin facade on a planked backing which was finely balanced to move easily. Picking up one of the guard's flashlights, I stepped inside, proving once again that I deserved that Dumb Bunny of the year award I was given at school.

The door clanged shut behind me.

Try as I may, I couldn't open it or locate the release mechanism which was undoubtedly there.

A bunch of cobwebs brushed my face making me jump and yelp. Hopefully, the trespasser had skedaddled.

"Phone. Use your phone, you silly girl," I said before realising pretty darn quickly that there was no reception. Some beastie ran across my feet, then another. Rats. I hated them. What to do? Trying to think rationally as I stamped my feet to discourage them, I pushed paper from my file into the minute gap that showed a sliver of light. I prayed that Ethan would spot it when he returned and come after me.

I couldn't stay here, not with these animals getting up close and far too friendly. I had no choice but to go down the stairs and follow the escape route to who knows where. It must emerge at some point otherwise Mr Intruder would not have used it. I decided to leave all the paperwork in my case there. The little beggars couldn't do too much damage by the time I returned and if I didn't make it back, that paperwork would be the last thing on my mind.

I called out one final time in the hope that the men had returned. Then, torch in hand I set off down the stone steps. In the momentary illumination from the flashlight, a metallic object glistened on one side of the earthen floor. Amid the layers of dust, it was incongruous; a polished ornament half-buried. Ignoring it as unimportant, I needed to concentrate. The steps had worn slippery edges under the powdery dirt of age. At least they were dry and I could hold on to the stones set out from the wall, a makeshift bannister. The Castle was constructed in the eighteenth century. Being this close to Holden and the borders, violence was a way of life back then. The word 'bereave' came from the three hundred year reign of the Border

Reivers, a lawless sect that preyed on Scot and Sassanach alike.

My footsteps resounded on the steps then became dull as I wove along a narrow tunnel with compressed earth and stoor beneath my feet. Distance was difficult to judge but here and there were notches for burning torches to illuminate the foreboding passage. Whoever built this fortified structure had both defence and, if the battle was lost, an escape plan for the gentry. Eventually, a glimmer of light was visible as I rounded a corner. More steps and I emerged into a dwelling of some description. the cotter's dwelling.

Although it was more decrepit than the Castle when Transudes began their renovation, the builders started here, making it sound and water-tight enough for storage of materials and electrical tools plus a generator. A packing crate marked Transudes lay opened near the concealed trapdoor through which I had exited.

Carefully, I made my exit into an especially dense part of the Tillymoor forest. It was becoming dark. Through the bushes and trees came the noise of a car starting – his getaway vehicle. I hadn't seen him and there'd be no video record of his face. From memory, there were tracks within the forest that he could use as an escape route away from Tillymoor.

Logic dictated that I'd found his way of entering and leaving Transudes undetected and that was enough. Yet I wanted more – a number plate at least. Wary of being seen, I crept towards the starter motor sound. Because the engine wasn't turning over, he kept trying the ignition. All he achieved was a slower whirring with each attempt, draining the battery until there was just a continual click.

His car was just ahead, the make and plate were easy to remember. If I were the intruder, I'd be legging it. He wasn't. Like a dog with a bone, he was determined to continue flogging the dead horsepower of his vehicle. Assuming he'd made a clean getaway, he opened the bonnet in a bizarre expectation that the battery would recharge.

I was strangely tired, closing my eyes despite the potential danger from this man. Any noise, a snapped twig and he'd realise I was here.

From my side, a whispered, "Kirsty? You OK?" Ethan and the guards had arrived, presumably following me through the tunnel. Thank goodness!

"Police are on their way, Mr Davis," the older one announced softly as I began to nod off again. I shook my head to clear the lethargy. "There's no sign of a weapon. Shall we deal with him?"

"Yes," Ethan responded without hesitation. His expression was that of pure hatred. "Then we'll find out what he has to say for himself."

◆　　◆　　◆　　◆

Upon arriving home, Gran was understandably concerned. I'd rung her to inform her of my delay. She surprised me by admitting that it wasn't unexpected.

"You and Tillymoor Castle are an accident waiting to happen, Kirsty. Apart, each of your existences would be uneventful, even mundane. But combine the two, like a match and petrol and the ensuing conflagration is an inevitability. The fact that you must realise, my child, is that it's far from over."

"Charming. Seems like we have lots to discuss. You order a meal. I'll be home in ten but I'll need a long shower before eating and talking. By the

99

end of tonight, I want answers from you, not enigmatic prophecies."

She laughed. "Same old Kirsty. Wanting to run before you can walk. I await our discussion with interest, lassie. See you soon."

♦   ♦   ♦   ♦

We began our heart-to-heart while eating. Alcohol was off the agenda; bad for the mind and soul, said my grandmother. To be fair, I was too fond of my wine these days therefore I agreed.

"The four of us being together isn't a coincidence, Kirsty. It's like roads coming from various unconnected villages meeting together at a roundabout."

"Four? Please explain." I took a spoonful of rice and tikka, ignoring the niceties of culinary behaviour. My home, my rules. All the mouthwash in the world couldn't get the taste of that hundred-year-old dust from my throat. A curry just might.

"You and me, naturally; Ethan and the Grey Lady. Sadly you're the catalyst, but you realised that, didn't you?"

"Yes. Events are triggered when I'm around The Castle and The Lake. Why?"

"Love makes you more sensitive, hormones and rampant emotions. Do you recall Mr Redcap, that gnome you talked to in the garden?"

"I didn't. I do now. Don't tell me he was real."

Gran laughed. It was good to hear that again, so full of life.

"Certainly not. Your imagination being shared with some pocket of energy and becoming real to your special sight. Same with ghosts, UFOs, so-called magic. Some can sense it, others not. Describe 'green' to me?"

100

Wow, talk about changing the subject. Gran was making a point, though. I played along. "Green is… green… halfway between yellow and blue, the colour of trees, the colour of that colander." I was digging a bottomless hole for myself here.

"Yet, it doesn't exist except in our mind. We see a particular wavelength of light and because Daddy said it was 'green' when we were a baby, our mind interprets it as green ever since. My green is different from your green but I can't prove it. I had cataract operations last year. They removed the yellowed lenses from these old eyes and put hard clear plastic ones in their places. First thing I noticed was how bright and vivid the colours were. My old green was something else, yet I'd had a magical transformation. It's fantastic but until those operations, I had no idea that this vivid world existed."

Thought-provoking but the point was made.

"What happened to Mr Redcap?" she asked.

"He faded and one day he wasn't there any longer. I couldn't hear him either."

Gran reached over to touch me. My childhood friend appeared again, gnome hat made of yellow petals and clothes of olive green. He was staring at me. I jumped. "Blinking hell. He's back."

"He was never gone. Your imagination plus a connection to the energies of nature. Gnomes are one thing, ghosts another. They're not from your imagination and they do exist. Say goodbye to your faerie friend."

I did, waving as a tear filled my eye. Gran took her hand away and he vanished.

"OK. Enough nostalgia. You're the key to solving the mystery of the Lake of Mists, your future and whether there will even be one. Ethan is involved with some extremely bad people, Kirsty. The trouble is, he doesn't realise it as yet, not fully. That's where you and I come in."

♦   ♦   ♦   ♦

Tillymoor was a nexus according to Gran. She showed me a map of ley lines, ancient energy trails where places like Stonehenge were constructed. Firstly, paranormal activity was at a high point with the return of people working in the Annexe for Transudes and with Ethan's family moving into Tillymoor Castle. From the distant past, the Grey Lady's spirit was manifesting more and more, drawing from the energy of people.

When I mentioned our intruder's dead car battery, my grandmother explained that Tillymoor wanted energy, any energy. People weren't in danger but they might feel tired. Maybe that was what happened to me in the forest. Car batteries were another energy source. It had been parked close to the Lake of Mists.

Secondly, I'd arrived. A Rain Whisperer and the Lake of Mists, a marriage made in Heaven. The trouble was a communication breakdown. That's where Ethan and Gran came in to join us together, or so Gran reasoned.

Unfortunately resolving the past turmoil of Tillymoor was under threat from the criminals of the present day. Two murders, computer records destroyed and that guy from earlier tonight, privy to the secret passages in the Castle and intent on subverting the investigation into the money laundering practices within Transudes.

The mastermind was a slippery fish, coated with Teflon as well. I'd already had the pleasure. Christian Wilczyca (she-wolf in Polish) now confirmed by Gran as the wolf that I should be very wary of. He was well-known to the police. The trouble was that he'd avoided being prosecuted thus far. If caught, his lackeys didn't implicate him, preferring to go to prison.

While we discussed this situation, DI Woolf rang. A coincidence of names thrown together as the ethereal presence of Tillymoor manifested itself. It was clear that my gran and the Detective Inspector had a close connection. The police woman explained that our intruder admitted to the previous acts of subversion at Transudes, including the destruction of Moira's computer and the main bank of computer records. He'd been given details of that secret entrance and had previously visited the Annexe as a computer engineer weeks ago. He denied being involved with the murders of Brodie and Mr Jenkins and refused to say who'd paid him to do this. For planting the explosives and detonating them remotely he was facing attempted murder but was unfazed by the implications.

That didn't surprise DI Woolf. "Some people have no conscience," she explained.

Once they'd finished the call, I tried to assimilate the information. "What do we do about this business partner? To catch him?"

"At the present, nothing," Gran answered. "To me, it's a matter of piecing together the dodgy accounts paper trail; the one he's at such pains to eradicate. If he wants them gone there's an obvious reason. Originally he tried to do it without drawing attention to it, now his sole recourse is intimidation: 'Back off or else'."

My despondency was evident because Gran immediately gave me an embrace. "Don't give up, love. You have your skills and we detectives have ours. Moreover, I have a strong suspicion that your talents, meagre that they are for now, might be useful against this person and his methods. Shall we make a start on your lessons? Rain Whispering One-oh-one."

Truthfully, Rain Whispering was pretty well what I did. Gran explained it and I asked what was special about it. As usual, I'd missed the point. The rain does listen, as I told Ethan that first soggy day we met, but it talks back as well. Not in words, mind, because that would be loop-de-Lou, but it responded to requests if they were said with sincerity and a gentle voice.

"Yeah, right," I replied on first hearing this. I mean, that I sensed ghosts and wee folk was OK but expecting the rain to do what you ask it to do nicely? In your dreams! "Gran. Are you becoming senile?"

"You cheeky so-and-so. But yes, probably. Let's go to the kitchen." She was off like a shot. I followed her, the floor tiles in there cold on my bare footsies.

"Dessert? I forgot. What would you...?"

"Button it, Kirsty. I'm going to show you what you can do." That was me well and truly put in my place. I stood by the tap as she turned it on, adjusting it to a fine stream.

Next, she rubbed a comb vigorously on her cardie sleeve, holding it an inch from the steady stream. It bent towards the comb, moving as Gran raised and lowered the comb.

I wasn't impressed. "Static electricity. Water molecules are affected by the charge, So what?"

"You try, Kirsty. Without the comb."

I put the tips of my fingers near the stream. Nothing happened.

"Now, ask the water to move. Encourage it as you would a child learning to ride a bike. Go on."

I felt ridiculous but I'd get no peace until I tried it. Speaking to the water, I kept glancing at Gran to gauge her approval or not. Then the water did a little jiggle. I was astounded. More whispers to it and within a minute I was able to direct it away from my fingers and towards them.

"Bloody hell!" I exclaimed without thinking.

Gran tisked very loudly, reminding me of those naughty times years ago when that same disapproving glare stopped me in my tracks.

"You have an affinity to water. At present this is a party trick. Your body might have static electricity in it that caused that. I'm no scientist. But it's a start to the person that you might become. It's late but there's one other thing I need to share with you. My research on Tillymoor. If you can manage bedtime reading, I'd suggest you do it."

"Why?" I was exhilarated by what I'd done with the water. Nothing could beat that. Yet realistically, I was dead tired. Gran said it was late but to me it was early: ten-thirty. I normally stayed up for another two hours and was one of those fortunate people who managed fine on five to six hours sleep.

Tonight was different.

On a day that had been filled with drama and revelations, her next words struck me as the root of this coming together of everything, the four of us: Gran, Ethan, me and the Grey Lady.

"It's all I could find out about Tillymoor Castle and specifically Mary Elizabeth Musgrave, the Grey Lady before she drowned. You, me and she... we're all related."

CHAPTER 10

That night, I had the history of Tillymoor to read. I also had the proposal for the Holden Megacity shopping mall to peruse before Ethan presented our bid to the authorities tomorrow afternoon.

In the end, I looked at neither.

The minute I curled up in bed, I was asleep. It wasn't a restful sleep though. Usually, we dream more at the end of the night in lighter REM (rapid eye movement) sleep. The deep sleep that we all usually experience after an hour or so eluded me. That was the revitalisation phase. What I had were dreams – horrid, upsetting dreams.

All about Tillymoor Castle.

It was as though I were there. I was the Lady of Tillymoor. I was also a prisoner of the despotic Laird, just another trophy to be displayed and coveted like those treasures he and his men looted from surrounding towns and churches. My sole opportunity for freedom was an hour each day to wander the Maze and around the newly constructed Lake which was the focal point of the grand estate. Other castles had moats to act as a barrier of defence against attack, the classic drawbridge and portcullis gate the sole entry to the fortified inner sanctum. The Laird regarded his vice-like grip on the surrounding rabble and other landowners so absolute that he did not need such defences, If an attack were made, he would act swiftly and decisively. Consequently, he built the Lake in place of a moat, or rather his men did. And Mary Elizabeth was permitted to promenade around it while the rest of the time she stayed imprisoned within the Castle walls.

I awoke drained and feeling as though I'd had two bottles of wine instead of none. My head ached like a morning-after hangover and my joints weren't great either.

Then, a mouthful away from my porridge breakfast, Gran mentioned my restless night.

"I heard these moans from your room but put that down to... well, you know. When the screaming began, I went to investigate. Your lights were on. I woke you and then waited until you drifted off again."

"I don't remember that. It was a nightmare. Mary Elizabeth." Instantly I regretted that. Gran would blame herself for mentioning the name just before bedtime. I had to reassure her. "It wasn't your revelation, Gran. Maybe I'm coming down with a bug. That dust in the tunnel was vile."

She accepted that with reservations, reminding me of the meal tonight with both of us at Shannon's and Bruce's. He could bring me up to date on his computer investigations. Reaching over, she put the back of her hand on my forehead.

"A bit warm. Do you feel hot?"

"If anything, I'm cold. I think I'll grab a cardigan. I can always remove it later."

◆　　◆　　◆　　◆

Arrival at the office didn't go as well as I expected. In the car park, I was met by Erin, returning to pick up her handbag and such. She'd then head home to recuperate. Her upper arm was bandaged.

"Goodness, Kirsty. You look worse than I feel and that's pretty rotten."

"Thanks, Erin. Just the way to brighten my morning. How are you? Truthfully?"

107

She'd heard of last night's drama. Every day brought more surprises for Transudes. Her injury was healing but it'd be several days until she returned to work. Reaching my office, I hardly put my case down before Ethan entered. He thanked me again for alerting him to the intruder. Last night, he and Heather had been upstairs in her room, wrapping presents for Ava's birthday in mid-September, hence the reason they'd not heard me shouting.

"How did you manage with the Megacity read-through, Kirsty?" he said after I shared details of the intruder's interrogation by the police.

Sheepishly, I replied that I hadn't had a chance to analyse it. He was disappointed. "You weren't injured, were you?" I said that I wasn't, staying clear of the discussion with Gran.

Although I could have made an excuse, I didn't.

"Please do it right away. Top priority. I want your best work on this, Miss November. We need an edge to secure this contract or Transudes..." He stopped, the implications of failure unspoken. "Do your best. We need that contract. I'll be back in two hours then I'm off. I'm taking Hamish from Planning. He's at least familiar with the logistics."

Closing the door, I was glad that he'd gone. My pretence to be one hundred per cent had drained what little energy I had. All he wanted was another overview of the twenty-eight-page proposal with a competitive bottom figure that would secure us the contract without crippling the company. Looking at the big picture was my strength and the reason he put his faith in me.

I told Samantha not to disturb me under pain of being unplugged then sat down with a pen, paper and the finished proposal. The first two paragraphs piqued my curiosity but that was it.

108

Then Ethan's angry voice startled me from my fitful slumber.

"What the hell are you playing at, Kirsty? Have you read anything at all?"

I stammered a dozy excuse yet he was having nothing to do with it. I'd let him down, big time.

"One thing I asked you to do and you choose to take forty-winks instead. I must have been mad to promote you. Totally mad! There are no second chances with me. I'm off now. Thanks for nothing."

Before I could stir and struggle back to wakefulness, he'd left for the lengthy drive to Holden. I had to stay awake and focus but my body was too weak. Going to the window, I watched as Hamish was asked to drive by Ethan. Watching him kicking the car tyre, I understood why. He was far too upset with me.

"Did you hear that, Samantha?" A rhetorical question but half the staff probably heard it.

"What can I do, Kirsty?"

"If I fall asleep wake me. Loud rock and roll but nothing by Wham." I did have some standards.

It was hard going. More than once, I began to drift off to slumberland, my eyelids closing. Doing this in such a state was insane but I had to. No revelations concerning the contract bid sprang to mind. That was until I noticed the site for the development. It was on the banks of the Eden near Rickerby. I recognised that name from my University of Griffith days many years ago.

"Damn. I remember that site," I exclaimed, conscious of Samantha's unseen hovering.

Me and a bunch of other students were there to protest at the development plans for an exclusive golf course and leisure centre complex. We wanted it for the ordinary people to be able to

109

enjoy the magical view down the hill to the Eden.

In the end, the plan failed to gain approval. By then, millions had been spent on a mandatory investigation for English Heritage. Building on virgin land was permitted, although firstly the area must be thoroughly investigated by people such as archaeology teams to ascertain that a car park wasn't built over an ancient Roman fort for example. The builder funds that investigation even though it might shut down any construction. That meant a calculated gamble to get a clean bill of health in order to go ahead. It was often slow, painstaking and expensive but a necessary evil from the point of view of any developer, often adding over a year to the timetable.

Transudes had budgeted two point eight million for that. No doubt, our competitors had too.

But why? It had already been done. I'd watched it from the protest sidelines. Later, I saw the report clearing the site for construction. Having another made no sense whatsoever. The Roman army wouldn't have left anything in the intervening period. Tourists yes, but not the Romans. I was aware that the report was done less than ten years earlier therefore a new one wasn't necessary.

"Samantha. Get me Griffith Council Planning on the phone." I cast my mind back to those alcohol-soaked Uni years. Like me, one of those passionate protesters had switched sides to the establishment enemy and was employed by the Council. "Ask for Harry Graham."

◆　　◆　　◆　　◆

Not long later, we had all the documentation I needed. By we, I meant Samantha as well.

Having an electronic interface that I could request information from and have it done without question was a big plus. Taking a deep breath, I phoned Ethan's mobile. Hamish was driving therefore no safety problems.

"What do you want, Kirsty? A lullaby?"

I expected a cold reception.

"I can save us three point one million pounds. Samantha's sending a revised proposal."

"I'm in no mood for –" he replied angrily.

By that time, I'd hung up.

Pacing around the room, I wandered over for my fifth cup of coffee. I was hyped on caffeine and would no doubt regret it. A quick dash to the Executive Washroom and I resumed pacing back and forth, my shoes discarded much earlier.

"Come on, Ethan. What are you?"

Finally, he rang back. Taking another deep breath, I answered on loudspeaker.

"Kirsty. Hamish and I are pulled up at the roadside. We've skimmed this twice. How did we miss this?"

"Griffith Council has the file. You're dealing with Holden Council. Lack of communication. Samantha's sent the historic significance report and I've incorporated the cost savings into our bottom line. You make certain that you two do the final presentation. It'll knock their socks off. Lots of red faces but it's solid. I talked to a mate in Council. He had a good laugh but won't gloat about it to the Holden Council crew until tomorrow. If I were you, I'd demand they give you the contract tonight before you leave. Embarrassment is a great motivator. I'm sure the Council wouldn't want it broadcast that they missed this, asking for a report that was already done."

Ethan and Hamish sniggered. "You're a

111

devious thinker, Kirsty. But you're right, Corporate blackmail —"

"Motivation, please. It's a less emotive term. Let me know how it goes. I'm going back to sleep now, if that's OK?"

"What I said earlier… sorry. Hope this makes up for it." He haltingly sang a few lines of a lullaby before hanging up.

Disconnecting the call, I addressed Samantha. "We did good, kiddo. Thank you."

"More coffee, Kirsty? Or shall I close the blinds and dim the lights?"

Yeah. The perfect PA, anticipating her boss's needs. Pity about the jokes but we could work on that. As for me, this lethargy was a real concern. It was this place, I was sure of it. And the ghosts here that I'd awakened.

♦   ♦   ♦   ♦

I was roused by the sound of the phone ringing. Illumination levels increased gradually.

"It's Mr Davis. You asked to put him through," Samantha explained.

"We got it, Kirsty. We bloody well got it! The minute Hamish casually mentioned that our research showed the historical survey was signed off, I could see it in their eyes. It took another hour of interrogation to rubber-stamp it but there was never any doubt. I let them postulate, gave them concessions as planned but that contract is now signed. What are you doing to celebrate?"

"Dinner with Bruce, Shannon and Gran." I yawned. Still not feeling up to driving.

"Have you just woken? What's up, Kirsty. This isn't like nyou."

"It's not. Just very drained." Similar to that

112

battery yesterday. A realisation began to take shape but I was too tired to follow it through. The other workers in the Castle offices and the Annexe were fine. Why me?

"Don't drive. Bruce is there, isn't he? Doing a track on that hacker? Get a lift with him. He can bring you back tomorrow as well. I pray you'll be better then."

I yawned again. "That makes sense. I'll give him a bell. Well done again. Perhaps we can celebrate together – another night though?"

Ethan hesitated. I'd forgotten. Ava was upset with me and that promise of an 'us' between Ethan and me was on hold until that was resolved.

"We shall see, Kirsty. We shall see."

I rang my friend on the Griffith Council to thank him. He'd gone out of his way to dredge up the relevant documents from archives, confirming what I recalled from back then. He was married with two kiddies. We reminisced a little over the 'good old days' and fellow students.

"Remember Josie?" said Harry. "She's a Chemistry professor at Cardiff these days. She was so easy to wind up, the ultimate millennial nerd. What was that puzzle you teased her with?"

I struggled, my brain's euphoria beginning to wear off. "Poisons? Oh yeah. Once a poison goes past its use-by-date, does it become less deadly or more?"

"Yes. That's the one. Good to catch up Kirsty. Don't be a stranger in future."

If all went to plan, I'd be seeing him from time to time, dealing with the politics of this massive development.

Having made arrangements for hitching a lift with Bruce, I again wondered about my tiredness. Normally sitting in the rain replenished my energy but there was no rain today. Maybe a shower in the bathroom attached here if this problem persisted?

That mention of poisons prompted an idea that might explain my problems – a long shot because no one else seemed affected. Maybe I was allergic to castle dust? "Samantha? Is there evidence of toxins in the Castle? Lead, asbestos, anything detrimental to my health?"

"Maybe. I can't say, Kirsty."

"What do you mean? You have access to Transudes Castle floor plans, before and after renovations, environmental reports."

"No. Those files have been deleted. I have present-day floor plans but nothing before Mr Davis assuming control of Transudes. Nor any record of how or who deleted them."

"Then your plans don't show an underground passage leading to the cotter's house to the northwest of the property?"

"No record exists."

While waiting for Bruce to call that he was ready, I swallowed my third paracetamol of the day. Maximum of four per twenty-four hours so I felt I was in control. I touched my neck and went to the mirror in the bathroom. My lymph glands appeared swollen but the way I felt…? Maybe it was my imagination.

Bruce called me soon afterwards as it was beginning to darken outside. The last thing I felt up to was a family get-together, however everyone was looking forward to it and Shannon was doing her speciality, roast beef with all the trimmings.

It was sad not to be using my new car. Realistically, me driving was dangerous, though. Bruce was never that talkative which was strange given that he was a lecturer. The way Shannon explained it was that he spoke too much during the day, therefore his brain was all talked out when he went home. I was grateful that I could doze on the drive. He'd tell us of his hacker discoveries soon enough.

As he turned the key in the front door, he commented, "You realise that you snore, Kirsty?"

"Snore? Rubbish. I breathe heavily, that's all," I replied wanly.

Gran was concerned about my reddened face. Shannon said the same. I explained that I'd been tired and had cranked up the room temperature as I was too cold. Shannon indicated that the heat rash was all over my body, noting my hands and legs.

"Maybe allergies," I offered, feeling as if I was part of an old circus sideshow.

"OK, but if you nod off again, don't fall face-first into the mashed potato and swede. Would you like red or white?"

"Nothing. Just coffee." I was determined to stay awake.

After telling everyone of the company's success at Holden, I shut up and let the others do the talking as I concentrated on enjoying the company and the meal. Shannon brought me a thick woolly jumper as I was shivering. It mussed up my hair but I was beyond caring.

Bruce's investigations, by their nature, were thorough but smooth. That man who'd done the damage to the computer systems wasn't the sole intruder into the records of accounts.

"There's a person on this side of the firewalls, playing with figures."

"What?" I asked, shocked. "In Accounts?"

"Certainly, within the Annexe. Your systems are much more secure than most, Kirsty but they're still vulnerable. It looks as though Ethan and his predecessor, Bartholomew Jenkins, took security seriously. There's a complex programme running that I couldn't access. It's confined to the Castle with separate links to e-mail and phone lines. No web access at all which is good. When I tried to investigate, a very sultry voice told me in no uncertain terms that access was denied."

I giggled. "That's Samantha. Ethan named her. Very sophisticated interactive system."

"She must be. She swore at me. It was kind of strange. Sounded like you when you're in a bad mood, but she was much sexier."

Gran and Shannon laughed at that. I didn't see the joke. "I can be sexy... I just never met the right man," I replied, defensively.

The conversation moved on to other things, Shannon's work, Gran's work, Mum and Dad. I half-followed it but I was intrigued by what Bruce said about the inside man or woman, presumably in cahoots with Christian, the dodgy guy with the Polish surname.

"Excuse me, Bruce. Sorry to interrupt. The person working at Transudes – could it have been Brodie Douglas, the man whose body was discovered in the Castle?"

"Not unless he's one of the undead." He was joking but it was too close for Shannon, Gran and me. Bruce knew nothing of our family's ability to see into the spirit world and wouldn't have approved. It was Shannon's secret and now wasn't the time to share that.

I was the first to speak. "Why? Because the illegal activity continued after he died?"

"Exactly. Stopped a few days ago though. Probably because that DI Woolf and I are snooping around the system. I'll brief you and Ethan

116

tomorrow on my findings and recommendations. I've already closed all the vulnerable access points from outside. Shutting down the money-laundering accounts too. I plan to freeze them but it's a very sophisticated arrangement. Hard to do even for a super-genius like me."

We laughed at that. It was true but modesty wasn't one of Bruce's most endearing traits.

Gran and I left not much later, her driving me home. We didn't stay for dessert, as I suspect in my dazed state, it was decided an early night for yours truly was in order.

◆　　◆　　◆　　◆

Another night of Tillymoor dreams, the same as the previous yet more intense. The smells were the worst – 'country smells' was the polite euphemism. The truth was, people in that era believed that washing caused disease and they avoided anything that approached modern hygiene. Mary Elizabeth was given a meal in her bedroom. She was tarted up and brought out from her confinement when required if there was a banquet or clan chieftains to impress – a trophy wife in the worst sense of the word.

As hoped, my morning shower did revitalise me although the stench of ancient Tillymoor clung to me. I tried to avoid Gran's fussing and entreaties to stay at home or visit a doctor. Tillymoor needed me. In retrospect, it was summonsing me, clouding my judgement. If I had looked in the mirror that morning, common sense would have prevailed and I would have sought medical help. Instead, I dispensed with the usual make-up routine and left my wet-tangled locks dry by themselves.

Once I made it to my refuge in the Castle,

everything would be fine. That's what I told myself.

I waited outside my house, with a scarf around my face, awaiting Bruce. As he arrived his first words were, "You look like a bloomin' vampire!"

Nothing more was spoken on the drive in.

"Just drop me out the front by the Lake, please," I asked Bruce.

Walking from the car park behind the Annexe area wasn't on the cards. As an Australian friend was prone to saying after a heavy night on the town, 'I feel as sick as a dead chook on the barbie'. That summed me up.

Bruce drove off with a promise that I'd call if I wished to go home to bed.

I started to walk up to the Castle steps. Then strangely, I found that I was heading to the Lake of Mists instead, coaxed there by an unseen presence whispering in my ear. I stood there, mere feet from the Lake's edge, staring out across the rippling waters to the Mists beyond. Time blurred, the Mists were eternal, gently swirling, easing then thickening in a bizarre pattern that wrapped the far side of the waters and surrounding trees in a blanket of white.

I took one step forward, then another until the water touched my feet. Then, as another mist closed around me, I sagged to the mown grass before beginning to shake all over. Voices. Frantic voices. Being moved. Blanket. Heather bending over me.

"Can't you stop her convulsing?"

Ethan frantic.

Lianne's voice. "I'm trying..."

"Paramedics on their way... that rash, it's petechial haemorrhaging."

"Damn it. What can we do?"

118

CHAPTER 11

As Mary, I was living an awful existence. The Laird – for that was what I must address him as – was despotic and jealous. If there were a grand banquet in the hall, I'd be instructed to wear the finest clothes adorned with jewels that he'd purloined. Once, a guest grabbed me and snatched the broach I wore, claiming it to be stolen from his mother on a raid where his parents were slain. The Laird listened to his rants demanding justice – then killed him amid festivities.

♦   ♦   ♦   ♦

I drfited in and out of consciousness in the hospital. I had a drip in my arm. Ethan and others visited but I was only dimly aware of their presence.

It was Saturday morning when I began to feel more like myself.

An elderly female doctor came to my bedside, accompanied by trainees. I was a celebrity but for the wrong reasons.

"RBF, Miss November. Rat Bite Fever. You're a lucky woman in one way at least. Rat Bite Fever's bacterial. There's just a couple of cases in Britain each year, mainly from pets. In that respect, you've been quite unfortunate. I gather there are rats where you work?"

In the secret passage on Monday night. The illness started within hours. I told her the circumstances.

"Unlikely. It takes a few days. There's a bite

119

mark on your neck. Vampires or an affectionate lover aside, I believe that's the culprit."

In the parking lot where I fell.

"As I said, very rare. We struggled to identify your infection. Sepsis was starting. It was touch and go. Did you realise you're allergic to penicillin?"

"No." That was a shock. I vaguely recalled waking up to loads of medical staff in a barely controlled panic. My throat was sore from whatever they had to do, a procedure I preferred not to dwell on.

"We used Erythromycin in the end. It was a close call."

Understanding the situation, at last, I asked if Ethan was aware of the potential danger to others. She explained that he was. Exterminators had been called in to eradicate the problem. The ultra-sonic deterrent used for all pests in the renovated parts of the Castle was being extended to ensure no recurrences of the problem happened.

Lying in bed in a less than flattering nightwear with a half dozen strangers staring at me intently wasn't a great experience. However, I owed my life to these people and their colleagues. The disinfectant I'd put on the bite wasn't enough to prevent the infection.

I was weak and guessed I'd lost a bit of weight which wasn't a bad thing. My joints ached and the purple dots over my skin were diminishing in size. Although I didn't want the nightmares back, I needed my sleep and so was pleased that, when I did nod off, it was restful for a change.

The private room was appreciated, probably due to the nature of my illness. When the staff weren't around, fussing as they did, it was lonely. Reading and Sudoku were difficult due to lack of concentration and the TV choices were diabolical. The hours were dragging by far too slowly.

Ethan's and Gran's visit that evening was much appreciated. Ethan thought it best not to bring Ava. He doubted she'd be allowed in even if she'd wanted to come. She'd sent a lovely card she made. He explained that her belligerent attitude was when she misunderstood a comment Heather made to me: that I had a boyfriend already. She'd taken a shine to me before that and felt betrayed. The card was promising as far as restoring our budding relationship.

My tenure in the new job had lasted two days so far and one of those was a near disaster. Ethan assured me that the office was surviving without me – barely. Another card was presented with over forty well-wishers signing – the entire office staff.

Standing up to put it on my bedside table, he kicked the drip trolley. "Rats!" he exclaimed in deference to women being present.

"Not my favourite animal at the moment, I'm afraid," I mentioned. "I trust that there won't be any other encounters of the furred kind?"

"No. Proper treatment this time. Even with the ultra-sonic deterrents oscillating at varying frequencies, the rats are adaptable. 'Nature's survival machines' the exterminator called them. With Tillymoor being old, it'll require ongoing monitoring. It's unusual for theml to bite people, though. Do you naturally attract rats – apart from me of course?"

I blushed, hoping the petechial spots weren't on my face, a point I hadn't considered before.

Gran had been unusually quiet, politely listening. She'd have her turn. I assumed that Ethan needed to get back to the Castle at least

121

to allow Heather some time with her husband.

"What about the police investigations, and Bruce's report?"

"We'll discuss that when you're better. There's nothing definite yet but progress is being made. Unfortunately, that guy who came after you is dead. An 'accident' in prison. What's that saying? Dead men tell no tales? The person behind this isn't taking any chances."

"You'll need a place to recuperate, Kirsty," Gran said, a change of subject for my benefit.

"Can you stay another week?" I asked.

"Sadly no, my sweet lassie. Commitments. I am a director of the company and must be in Edinburgh all this coming week. Ethan has kindly offered to have you at the Castle. Heather will help out and the District Nurses."

"That's very generous of you, although I'm wondering if you have an ulterior motive, Ethan?"

"Giving you a bed-bath?"

"Absolutely not what I meant, Mr Davis. I meant that I'll be on call to do work for Transudes, living on the premises. Not that I mind. I'm bored doing nothing here alld ay."

Ethan was taken aback at his faux-pas. Something about being close to each other brought out the cheekiness in us. I called him over so what I had to whisper was more private.

Taking the hint, Gran went to the window.

"Bed bath, no, Mr Davis. A double shower is a possibility though."

"Hmmm," he said, kissing the lobe of my ear.

Then he moved away declaring that it was time for him to leave. "Glad you're recovering, Kirsty. So's the company by the way. You're a clever girl. Beautiful too. And there's a special surprise in store for you back at the Castle."

After departing, Gran came over and pulled up a chair. She waited patiently as a nurse checked my blood pressure, temperature, and the drip.

"Ethan said I'm beautiful – am I Gran? I don't feel it. These spots…"

"Aren't on your face, love. And one of the nurses must have brushed your hair while you were sleeping. You snore, by the way, Kirsty. "

I was becoming tired of defending my sleep patterns. "It's heavy breathing, Gran."

"Thinking of Ethan, then?" my grandmother replied with a smirk. Ambling over to the window once more, she peered down.

"Expecting another visitor?" I asked.

"Yes. Another little surprise. One I have for you. I must apologise that your training has been cut short but until you regain your strength, it would be pointless and frustrating for us both. Fate brought the players together for whatever awaits you at Tillymoor yet she loves to frustrate us at the same time. A bite from a rodent, enough to scupper my attempts to open your eyes to your capabilities. That's why I reached out to another to watch over you. Who knows? Maybe that's part of the plan too, a fifth member of our elite band to protect the present and right the past."

"You're being very circumspect and mysterious, Gran. Speaking in riddles isn't you. Just come out and say whatever's going on."

She smiled, a glance now and then outside. "You're right. I sound like a cheap crime novelist dropping hints of the rest of the book unfolding. These are the facts as I understand them – Tillymoor has a connection to our family through Mary Elizabeth. Your dreams aren't simply dreams. Her ghost is reaching out to you and I suspect it's via those mists and the Lake."

Her pensive expression altered as she saw whoever she was expecting arrive in the car park. "Ahh. Voila. Our mysterious new teacher. She won't be long. Time enough for me to tell you of the present dangers: our criminal friend, Christian Wilczyca, with his foreign surname but as British as they come. He's been using Transudes to legitimise monies gained through illegal means. Big in export-import yet he conceals the stolen goods with shipments of the ordinary then sells to the highest bidder. The investigations of my agency and the police haven't revealed exactly what or where the goods are held as yet but..."

My brain was beginning to focus. "You suspect there's a trail within the accounts that he's killed and tried to destroy, the accounts at Transudes."

"Exactly."

A knock on the door heralded the coming of my new instructress. Having to go to Edinburgh before showing me my potential as a Rain Whisperer frustrated Gran therefore she'd found a surrogate to unlock my raw power. She trusted the newcomer although there was more to this handing over of responsibility than that. Gran, as always, had her reasons.

"Come in," she called out, an apprehensive mien crossing her ageing face. She was worried about my reaction.

The door opened, my heart rate increased as I stared at the visitor then Gran.

"Hello, Kirsty. Long time, no see."

My voice cracked, either from my sore throat where they'd put the breathing tube in, or from emotion, it didn't matter.

"Mum?"

CHAPTER 12

The woman I'd not seen in years gave a wan smile as she came over to take my hand. Gran came too, standing behind but by her side. Her hand rested on Mum's shoulders.

"I wasn't certain you'd recognise me. It's been a while." Mum leant over to kiss me but I flinched.

"I want to Mum, but I'm not sure how contagious this bug is."

"It's not," Gran interjected.

This time I was the one to reach out and embrace her.

The discussion that followed revealed the sequence of events that had led to this reunion.

Shannon and Gran had come immediately they'd heard I was in the hospital. They'd described my symptoms but it wasn't until they found the bite under my hair that the diagnosis was reached. Shannon had contacted Mum and Dad. She'd explained about Gran being with me. Mum insisted on coming notwithstanding Dad's crabby opposition. That was the final straw, and Mum was staying with Shannon and Bruce for the foreseeable future.

A lot of tearful discussions had resolved their long-held antipathy. Mum was gifted in seeing aspects of the supernatural but Dad had slowly eroded that from her through jealousy or wanting her to always do as he wanted. No one was sure. Once Shannon and I began to witness the 'beyond world' as Gran named it, he insisted that Mum back him up by dissuading us to ignore our heritage. Gran and Gramps objected to this and Mum was torn between husband or parents.

Dad had won – until this week. My illness was the deciding moment for Mum. And now she was to be my teacher in place of Gran. In a week, a better solution would be found for Mum's accommodation, however bonds between mother and daughter were rejoined for me as well as her.

By this time, I was quite puggled again, although elated that peace reigned again between Gran and my mother. She told me how proud she was of me with long overdue congratulations.

I must have nodded off before they left because one minute they were there and the next they were gone. The skies outside were darkening and I was hungry. My throat hurt too. My right shoulder ached as though I'd been given an injection. It didn't make sense as I had a drip attached and the drugs were given via that. Maybe I was sleeping funny. As I sat up to pour water from the carafe on my bedside table, I noticed a note resting there. It wasn't from them, though.

My hands shook as I saw the name at the bottom: Christian. He'd been in my room, snuck in when no one was watching. With the exception of Ethan, I was 'relatives visiting only' and he was no relation to me. It was hard to focus as I reread the thinly veiled threats he'd written. Nothing that would convict him as a blackmailer yet the message was clear: Back off or else.

He described my pretty neck which suggested that he could, if he wished, have strangled me in my bed. Naturally, he'd be wearing gloves and had ensured there was no sign of him being here. Yet that didn't suit his purposes. The investigation into his affairs would continue. By keeping me alive he could manipulate me. Gran was mentioned, Shannon too and her adoption plans. He'd done his homework alright.

Like the Reavers, striking at the vulnerable loved ones, he was in control, but control of what? The money-laundering was one thing, yet there was more that he was using Transudes for. My head and body weren't up to solving this conundrum. Realistically stopping the investigation wasn't anything I was able to achieve.

Then I wondered if he was playing the same sneaky games with others. Ethan perhaps, or Ethan's father? What was it Ethan said as I'd questioned him about Christian? Strange bedfellows? My mind was in a spin, unable to concentrate fully. The sole item that was real was the paper in my hands and the single sentence I kept returning to was the last one before his boastful signature, written so that I understood exactly who my enemy was:

Please give my best to Ethan Davis and his cute daughter. And his wife, Yvette, of course.

What a very strange thing to say. Yvette was deceased, wasn't she? I wasn't sure what to believe.

After that, even the staff noted a deterioration in me, mentally if not physically. The dreams returned. At one point I awoke shouting in fear as a nurse touched me. Other staff were called, struggling to calm me as my pulse and blood pressure was far too high due to my irrationality.

Ethan arrived. I heard him although he wasn't permitted to enter my room. Words such as 'concerned' and 'can't understand'. A reaction to a drug was suggested, different from the penicillin. Yet, as my drug regime hadn't altered, the mystery persisted. Gradually the symptoms abated and I was permitted to leave at last, weak, thin and quite subdued.

Ethan walked beside me as I was taken to his

car in a wheelchair. In the boot he had a bag from my home packed by Gran, Ava and Heather were waiting back at the Castle. I held the three Get Well cards Ava had drawn and painted.

"Can you turn the heating up please?" I asked once he'd carefully fitted my seat belt. Although he tried not to show it, he treated me like an invalid. I'd lost over ten pounds and my face was gaunt, my clothes hanging loosely. It was the muscle tone that was most noticeable to me. Debilitated summed up the new me.

"What day is it, please?"

"It's Tuesday, Kirsty," he replied, his peripheral vision touching me as he drove. Whatever we had in the way of affection was gone. Pity had taken its place,

"Which month."

"Early September." One week almost. It felt longer. "Your room's set up. The bunny pyjamas are washed and waiting."

I smiled. "My secret's out then. I guess you expected exotic nightwear?"

"Not really. I wear Star War ones myself. Yvette bought them as a joke before she... went away." His tone darkened and we drove on in silence. Was Yvette dead or was she perhaps missing, being held by Christian in a dungeon, forcing Ethan to comply with his wishes?

The thoughts of paranoia had lessened but as we drove up the long drive to Tillymoor they were merging with visions of the past. Yvette in a dungeon? What was wrong with me?

Ethan drove around to the front of Tillymoor Castle between the Castle and the Lake. The Annexe was further away yet they must have had a look-out as a lot of the staff came out to wave as I alighted from the car. Feebly, I waved back.

128

"I see that I still have a few friends left," I commented, pleased they'd made the effort.

"Quite a lot. Erin sends an e-mail to all departments with an update. She insisted on stepping up to do the basic tasks. Her arm's not a problem. She's in your office. Truth is, we continue to be plagued by problems from inside these offices. Bruce closed down the accounts where the money was haemorrhaging however he's not traced the perpetrator to the point the police have proof. It's all very frustrating."

I was trying to stand unaided. It wasn't easy. "That's one thing at least, Ethan. Can we go inside, please?"

"Absolutely." Heather and Ava came down the steps, arms outstretched. Ava was over-joyed to see me holding her lovely cards. They both took an elbow. I glanced back to the Lake of Mists wondering if the Grey Lady was spying on me from the water's edge. She wasn't. That said, her statue's eyes followed me, whether with contempt or hope, it was difficult to shake that sensation that the trauma shared with Tillymoor was far from over.

"It's going to be fantastic you being here, Kirsty. Daddy says you're poorly but we can play games, jigsaws and Monopoly and findies."

"She means hide and seek, Kirsty"

"Sounds lovely. I love games. It's just that…" I began until Heather leapt to my rescue.

"Remember what Daddy and I explained, poppet. Kirsty needs rest."

Ava's face became sad.

"We'll have a game later, sweetheart. I think I can manage a jigsaw."

On the slow, painful route to my room on the first floor, Ava and I continued our chat, her more than

129

me. She was pleased that I thought so much of her cards as I placed them on the contemporary dresser. Considering the facade and age of the building, like my space-age office the Transude re-imagined sleek interior was smart and beautifully charming. A top interior designer had been engaged. I'd seen his payment. Worth every penny. The walls were shades of grey with accent touches of a rich burgundy lending opulence to what was an otherwise a neutral, almost clinical palette.

"I'm very pleased that we're friends again," I pointed out as I sat in an armchair overlooking the Lake through high, narrow arched windows surrounded by stone.

Ethan's little girl was uncomfortable, casting her eyes down to the clenched hands at the front of her patterned dress. Then, as if accepting my words, she grinned back at me. "So am I, Kirsty."

◆　　◆　　◆　　◆

Ethan was fetching other suitcases from his car whereas Heather was off searching for a thicker duvet. I was feeling chilled still despite the clement weather outside and the temperature-controlled room. Although weak, the outward signs of my infection had abated. Crucially, my thoughts were clearer. Whatever I was meant to do in this supernatural nexus, I was determined to achieve it as quickly as I could, hopefully with Ethan at my side.

Ethan returned and was pleased when he noticed the two of us laughing at one of her jokes. He rested hands on both our shoulders.

"It's OK if you want to kiss each other, even though it's yukky," Ava told us, grinning.

130

"Should we, Miss November?"

"I must look a mess but if you want to, I won't object. Don't they say that a kiss makes it better?"

Tentatively at first, then with conviction, Ethan wrapped his arms around me then gazed into my eyes. "I love you, Raindrop Girl."

"I love you, Mr Ethan Davis."

Before I closed my eyes, I saw Heather ushering Ava out of the room, "We'll give you two privacy. Just remember, brother. No strenuous exercise with our guest for a week at least."

As the door closed, the kiss was magical, the sort that would leave any woman gasping. To me, it felt right, and now with Ava's blessing, it was the ultimate promise of things to come.

For the first time in a week, I could consider our future as a family – if that was a possibility.

◆　◆　◆　◆

I managed to eat the sumptuous meal that Heather prepared for me. It was lasagne and garlic bread – not everyone's idea of 'haute cuisine' but the taste was the thing. Rat Bite Fever affected every part of the body. Strangely that included my senses of smell and taste. I savoured each bite. Taking the prescribed tablets including oral anti-biotics was a necessary evil. Although Ava thought it amusing, Heather must have been a little uncomfortable at my effusive moans of pleasure as I ate. Ethan nudged my foot under the table.

"But this is sooo lovely," I responded by way of explanation after another prolonged "Mmmmm." Not very ladylike was the expression Mum always used when I behaved in a naughty way. She used that phrase far too often.

131

Heather offered seconds to me with a reproachful stare. I bit my lip. "Sorry, everyone. Must be the medication. This isn't me."

Heather softened that look. "I don't usually get compliments for my cooking. Hopefully, it's not the drugs. Oh, one thing, Kirsty. I forgot to mention. The hospital sent some other tablets. Appears they were overlooked. You take one in the morning."

Great. More of the horrid things. My tummy wasn't going to be happy. If they helped then so be it. I was much better, even had a wander to my office to catch up with Erin.

Ethan reached over to touch my forehead then take my hand in his. "Since your temperature's normal, you're on the mend. I recommend an early night, however. Don't rush your recovery."

"Will you tuck me in?"

"Only if you're not wearing those rabbit PJs."

Realising his mistake, he apologised, suggesting that the purple satin negligee was much closer to my style. My eyes opened wide until I remembered that he'd help Gran to pack my bags at home.

Heather saved the day by pre-empting additional mistakes. "My brother, dear Kirsty, Famous for foot in mouth syndrome. One day he'll learn but until then you'll have to make allowances."

That evening was a full moon. Whether the illumination shining on my face woke me about three or not, I was too wide awake to return to sleeping. Taking a booklet from the desk, I decided to record my thoughts on the situation with Transudes and the snippets of information which, once put together, might make sense.

That Ethan, Ava and I were finally moving forward together in a relationship buoyed me up.

132

Heather had left homemade shortbread in a tin if I became peckish. The sugar rush might not be good for relaxing me, nevertheless, energy was required if I were to improve. I chose to go for a moonlight walk to the Lake.

Shoes on and with a blanket against any nighttime chill, I negotiated the stairwell carefully, holding onto the bannister for dear life with each step. The alarm deactivated, I went out the front. The exterior lights merged with the moon's glow to give the Lake of Mists a diaphanous aspect, muted colours accentuating the tendrils of haze reaching out from the watery surface. Moths danced as the chorus of insects and owls continued. A stronger light dazzled me momentarily as one of the guards appeared. I half-expected to be challenged. Ethan was taking security seriously.

"Oh, it's you Miss November. Let me assist you down them steps."

"Thanks, Duncan. Not that steady on my feet."

He sprinted up the stone steps to help me descend and across to the seat facing the Lake. The smell of the freshly mown grass was intoxicating.

"Just hold onto the bench, please, and I'll get the cushions from the storage bin. Just take two ticks. The seat's wet and no one wants you getting sick again, 'specially me." He returned, allowing me to sit in comfort. Then he returned to the patrol. I was alone on my bench, no rain, no people, just me and the night and the Lake of Mists drawing me to it in a way I'd never experienced before.

I wasn't cold but the Mist was. I could tell. In a way, it was similar to breaths of fog that we see on a crisp, chilled morn. The waters had their

133

own life and the Mists were their breath. Changes happened to me as fingers of the vapour reached out towards me. I wasn't sure how long I sat there at one with the cloud before my eyes.

Then she came, a spectre standing on the lawn a few yards to my left. The Grey Lady.

Her cloak was draped over her shoulders yet the hood was pulled back, exposing her face and neatly brushed hair. She didn't acknowledge me in any way. We were two figures under the golden glow of the moon, our attention on that living fog before us. As she was marginally in front of me, I decided to study the apparition purely from curiosity.

No one had seen her face as the hood concealed her features. Gently waving branches of trees were visible through the phantom form. Alive, she must have been beautiful at an early age but living at Tillymoor under the despotic regime of the Laird, that vibrancy and kindness had left Mary Elizabeth. She was a sad, abandoned soul when she passed from life to the limbo in which her ghost was trapped.

I studied her until tears began to run down my cheeks. What did she want from me? As if realising our time was limited, Mary Elizabeth pulled the cowl over her head, resuming that iconic pose of the statue. Then she lifted one arm. The loose sleeve fell away revealing the emaciated hand and wrist. A single finger pointed and I stared to find out the object of her gesture.

Footsteps on the gravel. Someone running behind. "Miss November? Are you all right?" Duncan was frantic.

I turned to him calling back that I was fine.

The Lady vanished leaving a panicked guard shining his torch all about me. "It was her, wasn't it? The Grey Lady? I seen her disappear. Did she hurt you, Miss?"

"No, Duncan. We were simply... admiring the view. Did you say you saw her?"

"Why yes. This is the fourth time. She's not dangerous, is she?"

"No. She's just a ghost, standing guard, like you in her fashion. It's not the dead we should fear. Oh, and please don't mention the ghost to Ethan. He doesn't accept that they exist. I'm returning to bed. Can you help me?"

"Certainly, Miss November. That's what I'm here for."

As I pushed myself up from the cushion, the air stirred as the breeze became suddenly stronger.

Duncan stared at the sky as grey clouds masked the moon. "Weather's changing. Rain's coming, I bet. What's that saying? It's an ill wind that blows...?"

"Nobody any good."

He took my elbow, insisting I keep the blanket wrapped around me and over my head. It was when we passed by the life-sized statue that he noticed the blanket colour and the uncanny mirror image of me in the protective material.

"Well, fancy that, Miss November. Two Grey Ladies together, you and she."

I gasped. He was correct, the hood, the loose sleeves, the hair. I was the Grey Lady tonight even down to the thin arms.

She'd become a prisoner of the Castle and died here. Was the curse of Tillymoor searching for another victim? The man chasing Ava and me? Then the rat bite and subsequent infection. Would it be third time unlucky and I'd find my spirit out there wandering around the Lake of Mists with Mary by my side?

CHAPTER 13

Back in my bed, I snuggled up under the warm duvet, intent on recording all that had happened, including my thoughts. The ongoing saga with the Grey Lady wasn't a priority to me. Whatever she planned would be revealed in time.

Christian, his not-so veiled threats to the safety of Ethan's family and mine was more important. He had a spy on the inside and I was certain they were working in Transudes to divert attention from his actions. Ethan's private security officers made entry from outside harder and that tunnel from the house into the Castle was now blocked off, the secret door sealed good and proper according to Ethan. I believed that, safe in here, nothing bad could happen – which showed how stupid and naïve I was.

I'd play games with Ava today. The non-strenuous sort. At least I was on the improve. Thinking about it, Ethan still hadn't shown me that surprise he promised at the hospital. I'd remind him today.

The rain arrived in force but there was no sitting outside for me. I made the effort to join the others at breakfast, freshly washed and dressed. It took longer than normal but I had to make the effort. This lounging around didn't suit me.

Heather made breakfast and supplied me with enough tablets to make me rattle as I walked.

"That's the new one from the hospital," she explained, as I popped it into my mouth with a mouthful of pineapple juice to wash it down. I felt very guilty imposing on the family. At the very least I'd help with the washing up.

136

"Green's bad for you, Kirsty," Ava advised, her first words since she'd wished me good morning.

Ethan laughed. "Sorry, Ava's going through a colour phase with food. Green's the latest."

"No, it's not, Daddy. I like peas and beans and 'sparagus."

Heather stepped in. "She does, too, Ethan. Orange is the new green this month."

"Yeah. Orange carrots are super-yukky. Daddy."

Ethan and I were puzzled. "Ava. Why do you think that green's bad?"

"Not all green, Kirsty. Just that tablet."

"You do understand that the doctors want her to have it, to make Kirsty better?" Heather explained.

I thought no more of it as I washed and dried the china later. Heather stacked them away. Once finished, I wasn't feeling great. Ava skipped in with a jigsaw box in her hand and an optimistic gleam in her gorgeous blue eyes. That was the perfect excuse to sit in the large lounge, the coffee table in front of us. Ava snuggled up by my side and tipped the pieces out for us.

"A hundred pieces?" I exclaimed, reading the box top. It was of a castle with a princess and knight on a horse. "Can you count that high?"

She gave me a cheeky, endearing smile. "Maybe not. But you can, Kirsty."

We began to play. Although I was happy to indulge her at first, my gaze began to wander around the room. A wedding photo intrigued me. I ambled over to examine it. Ava joined me.

"That's my mummy. She's very beautiful, isn't she, Kirsty?"

"Yes. Very." My response was automatic. I picked it up to examine her better. Ringlets of gold, a cherubic smiling face. She was too attractive. What chance did I have competing with her? She'd never grow old, never develop wrinkles around her eyes. She'd always be his first love and Ava's mother. Always. And what if she was alive and held a prisoner by Christian, forcing Ethan to hide his criminal deeds? What was I then? A momentary dalliance until Ethan and she were reunited?

Replacing the photo without breaking the frame took all of my self-control. Even then, my teeth gnashed together. Ava was staring at me as though I behaving strangely. How dare she? I wasn't the one cheating with the jigsaw, stealing my spaces.

Hold on. That couldn't be right. We weren't competing with one another. What was I thinking?

I relaxed, unclenching my fists.

Considering her youth, Ava was remarkably mature. Emphatic too.

"It's the green, Kirsty. This isn't you, being angry. Do you want to come to my bedroom and see my treasures: the broach and necklace what I found? They're really shiny. I want you to see them 'cause you're my friend. Then you can have a sleep."

"Yes, Ava. I'd like that. I'm sorry if I scared you." The angriness and feeling that the world was closing in on me was still there yet if I put all of my attention into Ava, the best part of my life...

She held my hand as I slowly walked up the winding stairs, choosing the outside curve where the stairs were widest, in case I stumbled or... or if I was pushed. But who wanted to push me? Christian? He wasn't here – was he? Maybe Ethan or Heather intent on stopping me telling the world that Yvette was in trouble.

"Just a few extra steps, Kirsty. You'll really love

my bedroom. Just wait until you see it."

I'd stopped, furtively glancing everywhere. The fear was overwhelming.

"There's no one else there, Kirsty. I won't hurt you. Come on."

"Yes… Yes, you're right. You won't hurt me."

But what if she did? What if she were part of it? I pulled my hand from hers and clung onto the bannister. Her voice was imploring me to keep going up. It was blurry and the floor was moving. I started to fall.

"Gotcha!" Ethan's voice shocked me. I tried to pull away then fell into his arms. "What were you thinking? Good thing I heard your screams."

Screams? I couldn't recall shouting. He was making it up, trying to confuse me. My blurred vision was clearing and the twitchiness subsiding. Ethan was holding me close and stroking my hair and my shoulders. The bite on my neck remained sore and every time his hand ran over it, it hurt. More than that, it was bringing me back to reality. Pain was pushing back the sensations of fear.

He was not my enemy. No one was, apart from Christian. How could I have thought that?

By now we were at the top of the stairs. Several office staff were watching as if I were a mad, demented woman. I probably was. Nothing was clear as my thoughts danced between unrelated aspects of everything. Trying to concentrate on a single idea was impossible, yet this morning outside at the Lake, my mind was clear. I'd written my ideas down. Perhaps if I reread them?

"Let's get you to your room, Kirsty. Heather will fetch a drink for you, to relax you. You pushed yourself too much, going outside last night. Duncan informed me."

Duncan? Then he was in on it too. Stopping me

from saving Yvette. No! Focus, girl. Focus...

"Ava wanted to show me... show me something. A broach and necklace she picked up. Her treasures? Yes, treasures." Through the fogginess of my mind, or what remained of it, I noted Erin staring intensely at Ava. I wasn't sure but I thought that Ethan also witnessed the older girl's expression.

"Kirsty, you can play with Ava another day."

"Yes, my room. Are you going to tuck me in, Mr big-strong man, Mister Davis? That would be so looovely."

Conscious of the gathering crowd, Ethan suggested that they return to their jobs leaving Heather, Ava and Ethan with me.

"Sorry," I pouted. But why should I be sorry? They were the ones I couldn't trust.

Heather was hugging Ava to her side, protectively.

"It's not her fault, Aunty. It's the green."

Ethan was upset by my words, especially as I'd said them near his employees. His and my credibility were in tatters. They escorted me to my room, instructing Ava to go to hers and lock the door. Why should she? I'd never hurt her, Never. Then I thought back to the stairs. Did I stumble or was I pushed?

Between them, they laid me out. Ethan sat on the side of the bed, caressing my head and cheek. "What is wrong with you, love? It doesn't make sense. You were fine earlier. Perhaps we should take you back to the hospital?"

"No. Don't. Christian wassh there. Let me shtay with you. Shafe here. Shorry for what I shaid."

I spoke softly as I curled up into a foetal position and whimpered. He kept his hand on me.

Ethan's sister returned with something to calm

me. It worked but I stirred later when they returned to check. The curtains were closed but I was aware enough to hear their muted conversation.

"She's a gentle, kind woman, Ethan, but this... we didn't sign on for this." Heather was concerned but not merely for me.

Ethan replied, "There's a big problem, sis. She was absolutely fine this morning. But you're right. Ava's our priority, not a..."

I thought he was about to say mad-woman yet thankfully he didn't.

They stood in the shadows considering options. It was Heather who finally spoke next.

"Her mother rang today. I was expecting her to step up and take responsibility but after ten minutes it was clear she's a mess herself. Just split up from husband."

Another lengthy pause.

"I'll bring her food up later. See how she is, but it's best if we keep her away from Ava until we discover what's happening, Ethan. As you say, it doesn't make sense."

"She mentioned one thing earlier. I believe Christian visited her in the hospital. Threatened her. But that doesn't explain this changeable paranoia. Ava told me that Kirsty thinks Yvette's alive. Hold on. She was writing her thoughts in that book by the bed. Perhaps I should read it?"

"Ethan. That's private. You shouldn't. She might not forgive you."

I heard him move to the bedside then withdraw. "If there are clues here, I must find out. And if she hates me..."

I was too groggy to move or speak and by now, the pillow was soaking from my tears. Everything was going wrong with my life. I wanted him to take me in his arms, kiss me and tell me it was going to be alright, but he didn't. He was too scared.

Love never was enough.

♦   ♦   ♦   ♦

The nightmares returned. As Mary Elizabeth, I was faced with an eternal life of imprisonment and abuse at the hands of the Laird. Strutting around or riding in his armour as the self-proclaimed Knight of Tillymoor, he lorded it over everyone as a cruel, cowardly beast. My walks in the Castle grounds were less frequent although I had a new reason to anticipate them. Having dropped a glove, a peasant tending the grounds rushed to retrieve then hand it to me. As our eyes met, I understood that he sensed my pain. I thanked him as I was wont to do for the smallest of kind mercies, then on impulse, requested his name.

"Hector, my Lady."

"Then thanks be unto you, Hector. Perhaps we shall meet again?"

He doffed his cap and withdrew.

I relished further encounters although most occasions outside in the cold, dismal winter found me sorely disappointed for the man called Hector was oft engaged elsewhere on the estate. The drudgery of my existence always was lifted momentarily whenever I did sight his smiling face.

The grand balls and festivities at Tillymoor were less o'er the winter months, a combination of the weather most intemperate and the fear from other landowners that they might incur the Laird's vicious ire.

On one March day, I espied a spray of daffodils on the worn path encompassing Lake, The morn mists had risen and the chilled waters were bathed in the morning sun.

I clasped my grey cloak around me before kneeling to retrieve the golden flowers then slyly I hid most of them within the folds of my cloak. Hector had stopped his labours momentarily to catch my eye. They were his gift and quite precious because of that.

That I could admire the blooms and freshly scythed grass on my Laird's domain was acceptable, a brief respite in my despondent life. I must never take anything of beauty back to my cell. Consequently, I discarded a single dew-touched flower on the steps when requested and returned to my windowless prison, clutching the other rays of sunshine lovingly to my bosom.

Over the following days, I stole glances at the sunshine yellow gifts from Hector when err I could. Having them with me, bright colours of nature most radiant, saddened me. For it is true. To have a touch of Heaven in Hell makes it bleaker still.

◆　◆　◆　◆

I awoke around three, refreshed despite the bad dreams. It was the overwhelming despair felt by Mary Elizabeth that enveloped me, far more intense than any normal bad dream. Although it lingered there was an undercurrent of love too that sustained Mary, the knowledge that Hector adored her, albeit from afar. Contact between them was forbidden, the merest hint of another man throwing the Laird into such a rage of jealousy, that both their miserable lives might be forfeit. Was this why she walked into the Lake that dreadful night, never to be seen alive again?

The moon was bright outside. My head was clear and my strength was returning. What had screwed my mind up so much yesterday? The

143

thoughts I'd experience, my actions, frightening Ava like that. All were unforgivable. I reached for my book to record the latest but it wasn't there. Then I remembered. Ethan had taken it.

Dressing, I stole quietly out of the room and descended the stairs, unlocking the door to return to the sanctuary of my Lake. Would ghostly Mary Elizabeth be there? What on earth did she want with me, in any case? It wasn't as if I could ease her misery yet here she was, reaching out to me across the centuries.

Duncan was awaiting me, once again assisting me down the steps. He brought the blanket and cushion for me to sit on, making certain that I was comfortable before meeting up with his fellow guard and the dog. Within minutes, I was alone with the noisy nighttime creatures my sole company. Reflecting on the events of the past day was far from pleasant. I'd behaved abominably.

A rustle behind me, footsteps. I smelt him well before he came to my front, taking care not to scare me. "You realised it was me?"

"After-shave. Less is more, Mr Davis. I assume Duncan contacted you to advise you I was up and about. Come to join me?"

"Depends. Are you Miss Jekyll or Miss Hyde tonight?"

I giggled at that. "Hopefully Miss Jekyll but with this full moon you never can guess."

"I brought a sprig of garlic. Just in case."

"That's for vampires, Mr Dozy. Nevertheless, I do have a bite on my neck. The start of my problems. To answer your question, I'm normal at the moment. Well, for me."

Ethan reached around me to pull my body close to his. He snuggled under the blanket and nuzzled my ear lobe. Tingles filled my body as I

144

pressed my lips against his.

"I'm so sorry," I whispered, as I pulled away, the emotion making me cry.

"Why? It's not your fault, love. Someone is doing this to you and Christian is my best bet. I... I read your journal – as much as I was able. Your scribble is virtually illegible."

"Yeah, but truthfully, I didn't write it for you. Then again, possibly I did. I had to let you understand what I suspected."

Another kiss as he wiped the dampness from my cheeks.

"Heather checked with the hospital. You didn't imagine it. Christian was there. CCTV. He said he was your brother. Furthermore, there was a syringe in the waste-paper bin. Totally against hospital procedures. They rang the office to warn them but nobody passed the message on to us."

I gasped a sigh of relief.

As his words sank in, the last bit stirred my anger. "I don't suppose they have a record of who they talked to?"

"Afraid not, precious. I have my suspicions and, from reading your scrawled ideas, so do you. The lovely Erin. You astutely pointed out that the cyber sabotage stopped the day she was hospitalised from the explosion."

"Yes, but she was injured. Hardly the brightest thing for a villain to do. Nevertheless, you suspect the same but we need more than conjecture. We need proof. This sickness thing, my paranoia and the rest. If Christian gave me an injection of a hallucinogen while asleep in hospital it should have worn off long ago. Yet it didn't. Yesterday I was a space cadet visiting other worlds. Everyone was against me. I believed that your wife was alive and you were being blackmailed, for Heaven's sake! I can't blame you and Heather for wanting me gone from your lives."

he gave a wry smile in the moonlight. "You overheard us? Fair enough. And yes, I was aware of you behaving as though you were on certain nasty drugs. Even looked them up. But if Erin's involved, how was she injecting you again? You've not seen her and I've ensured our part of the Castle is secure from workers and intruders alike. By the way, your Samantha is missing you."

Could a machine miss me? Why not? In Tillymoor Castle the impossible appeared to be quite easily reached.

I sat and stared at the wispy fog before us, the same fog that Mary Elizabeth seemed to point to last night. I wondered if she were around and, if so, would she approve of me and my Ethan being cosied up together. All she had of Hector were a few daffodils and a smile.

We sat like that under the stars, kissing often, with whispered words of love in between. Ethan told me of the birds we heard and we watched as frogs hopped across the grass. As it began to rain, I ran my hands over his naked chest under his shirt and coat. "Deja vu all over again. It's how we met, my love, in the rain."

"Don't remind me. I am not getting soaked again. Besides, we both need our beauty sleep. We must get you inside. Make sure you don't catch a cold. Anyway, big day tomorrow."

"Today," I corrected, happy to return to bed. "It's four-forty. Care to join me? I can do with another cuddle."

We were hurrying back to the Castle steps, the falling rain glistening in the floodlights before us. Ethan held the blanket over our heads.

"No, not tonight," he replied, breathing hard.

"I've too much on my mind to give you the attention you deserve. Plus, you are convalescing. If you're feeling frisky, perhaps you're well enough to be back at work?"

"I intend to start tomorrow. See how it goes."

Yeah, I asked myself. Provided that mysterious condition didn't strike me again.

◆　　◆　　◆　　◆

All of my spots had gone when I showered. I was refreshed and ready for the day. The antibiotics had done their job but I had to complete the course.

"You two look refreshed," said Heather, a grin betraying her suspicions. Ava was engrossed in her peanut butter on toast, oblivious to the amount all over her elfin face.

"You're a slaister," I told her, tickling her chin. She continued munching away.

Heather translated. Although Ethan had been born here, Ava was an 'outwith', technically an outsider. "Kirsty means that you're a messy grub, Ava."

Ava gave a huge peanut-buttery grin. "That's a good thing, Kirsty. 'Cause yukky grubs turn into pretty buttyflies and go from flower to flower. I'd like that."

I ruffled her hair before wandering over to the stove. "Here. Let me do that for you, Heather. You sit and be waited on for a change."

I'd prepare their breakfast and have muesli and yoghurt plus orange. The adults could have the full monty as Heather had already begun the cooking. When I did sit, I tried to ignore the plethora of tablets in front of me.

As Ava would say, 'Yukky'. She asked to be

excused, presumably to clean her face and hands. That was quite grown up, I thought, but not having any kiddies of that age in my small circle of friends, I had no idea of normal. She returned with a rattling orange Jacob's Cracker box.

"What do you have there, poppet?" Heather asked, stopping her eating long enough to wipe an errant crumb of sticky toast from Ava's otherwise clean face.

"It's my Treasure Box, Auntie Heather. I wanted to show Kirsty yesterday but she became poorly." Accents and dialects weren't usually a problem to me but her use of 'poorly' instead of ill or sickly reminded me that she'd been brought up in Manchester. Likewise, the way that Ethan said 'police' and quite a few other words was quaint. Heather, living locally all of her life at least spoke properly, to my ear.

Ethan explained, "She's a born collector, like her late mother. Anything small and shiny. Ava, we'll have a look after breakfast, OK?"

"But, Daddy..."

"After breakfast, pumpkin." He was firm when he wanted to be but otherwise, he and Heather doted on her.

As mature as she was, Ava pouted a little angrily. I wouldn't undermine Ethan but a quick tickle changed her upside-down mouth to a grin again. My eyes returned to the plate by the muesli bowl. Five tablets. I couldn't put it off any longer.

"That green one is bad for you, Kirsty," Ava said, serious and agitated. This carry on again.

"Why is it bad for me, Ava?"

"I dunno. The lady told me." My question confused her and she backed down, doubting her own adamant warning. I lifted it to my mouth.

148

"Wait, Kirsty. Put it down, please."

Now it was Heather showing uncharacteristic alarm. Immediately I put the green tablet on the plate, she relaxed. Staring all around and standing to check behind her, she asked us what had just happened.

Ethan took her trembling hand. "What's going on, Heather? You just shouted a warning about that pill. Don't you remember?"

Her eyes betrayed the truth. She didn't recall her actions. Moreover, I felt it also. The tablet. It was as though I was being protected through others, but by whom? The Grey Lady, or some other force within these castle walls?

"Excuse me, Heather. You mentioned that those green tablets were sent by the hospital."

"Why, yes. Your name and the dosage are on the label." As a group, we compared the bottles after retrieving them from high in the cupboard out of Ava's reach. All the others had typed labels, this one handwritten. The printed logo for the hospital was the same.

"We should verify this. Perhaps that's the cause of your distress yesterday, Kirsty?"

"Makes sense. You said they were delivered, Heather. Can you describe the courier?"

"No need. It was Erin. She'd signed for them then brought them to me."

"Erin," Ethan and I said at the same time.

I put the green medication back into the bottle, sealed it and washed my hands. Heather did the same to hers. We'd pass the offending tabs onto DI Woolf for analysis. Christian and Erin were doubtless working together, those tablets designed to distract us all from investigations and destroy my credibility. I'd have to ring Gran and Mum, make certain that they were safe from

149

his underhand threats. But why? His money-laundering operation was all but scuppered even if he'd made sure he wasn't linked to it any longer. There must be more to his involvement with Transudes and this Castle.

In the meantime, I owed Ava and Heather a lot. Taking that tablet would have brought me another day of confusion. No thanks.

"Ava. You did a really good thing warning me about that nasty green tablet. I should have listened to you yesterday and I'm sorry. Can I see your treasures now, please?"

Heather and Ethan gathered around as she opened the box. We were speechless, couldn't believe what was inside. Ethan said, "Who would have guessed they were here? At least that explains Christian's interest in Tillymoor."

I examined the ruby-encrusted broach. Ava's Treasure Box had very precious treasures indeed.

CHAPTER 14

Although tired and conscious of my gaunt appearance, I felt positive about the future. I played with Ava, completing the jigsaw, the breakfast dishes were stacked away and meat was thawing for tonight's dinner. We sat around, awaiting the evil Erin to make her move.

Ethan suspected that she'd guessed about Ava's treasures and was going to steal them. A camera was set up to monitor Ava's room. Any move to enter it would implicate her completely as all staff, apart from yours-truly, were forbidden to enter the private rooms of the Castle.

Sitting with the TV showing Ava's cartoons, I exchanged family secrets with Heather. Mine wasn't the only one with skeletons in the cupboard. Their father wasn't squeaky clean, Knighthood or not. We bonded well, she and I.

"You realise that I first brought you to my brother's attention. Since Yvette passed away, he's been a morose man, struggling at times to care for himself and Ava. I'm a bit sneaky too, Kirsty. Well, not so much sneaky, as a woman who wanders around the Annexe and the Castle without intruding. A phantom spy for Ethan."

"Tillymoor has its share of those already, Heather. One more...?"

"True enough. Not that I was spying. Simply noting little things like your row with Moira the day you and he met in the rain. I realised that you were the brains behind some of those clever ideas and mentioned it to him. The fact that you were gorgeous was a bonus. Up until then, he was frustrated with recruiting for your job."

"I owe you, then. Thanks very much."

She laughed loudly enough for Ava to twist her head to eye us. "Don't be daft. I have an agenda, too. I have my own life and helping out here while Ava's on holiday isn't part of my long-term plans. Two birds, one stone? Unless you or Ethan are objecting."

I understood. "We're not. I was afraid that I stepped on your toes."

"You're nowhere near Auntie's toes," Ava piped up. Little Miss Big-Ears. We'd have to watch what we said with her nearby.

Heather answered. "It's an expression, poppet. It means... I'll tell you later."

Ave returned to the TV, lying on the carpet. She propped her head on hands, elbows on the floor. "That's what you always say, Auntie. How am I even learn to be growed up if no one tells me

151

nothing? It's awfully, awfully frustrating."

"That's us told off," I giggled with a wink to my friend. Heather smiled in agreement.

◆   ◆   ◆   ◆

Over the following hours, Ethan brought me paperwork, suggesting that I do what I could and that I'd need all of my energy later.

"Whatever for, Mr Davis?" I replied, coquettishly.

Ethan went bright pink. "I meant dealing with the police if we catch Erin in the act? Not what you were suggesting," he replied.

Heather commented, "My brother is so easy to wind up. I have to apologise for him."

"You ladies do realise that I can hear yo– Oops, wait up. Erin's on the move."

Sure enough, we watched as Erin approached Ava's room. She unzipped a case and knelt by the door handle.

"Is that...?" I wondered aloud.

"A lock-pick." Ethan sneered. "She's come prepared, the enterprising so-and-so. Shall we?"

"All this is being recorded?" Heather asked.

"Oh yes. In glorious high-definition colour and Dolby stereo surround sound on two separate cameras," he replied. "I want a word with her before the police arrive."

"As do I, Ethan," I said. "She messed with my mind and I want to know exactly why."

"Shall we, ladies? I've buzzed the guards on the walkie-talkie. They're on their way."

◆   ◆   ◆   ◆

Erin was in Ava's room by the time the five of us arrived. She believed that we were busy elsewhere because that's what had Ethan mentioned earlier in passing.

"Breaking and entering is much better on a charge sheet than 'I'm innocent of any wrong-doing, simply admiring the doorknob'," Ethan declared sternly.

"Mr Davis!" she startled, trying to cover up her intrusion. "I noticed the door was open and thought there might be a problem. Is Ava alright?"

Whether that was a not-so veiled threat or not, the lack of response told her she was in trouble.

"Very well. You've caught me. No point trying to run. I wouldn't get far with this arm, would I?"

I broke our combined silences. "Yes, Erin. That puzzled us for days. You were the sole person injured when Moira's computer exploded. Was that to throw us off your pongy Eau de Pound Shoppe scent?"

That brought rage to her eyes, her Buffy smile vanishing as her true nature flowed like venom from a snake's fangs.

"How dare you berate me, you sanctimonious weirdo! Seeing ghosties, getting drenched whenever you can and now cosied up to the Big Boss, flashing your cleavage. You make me puke! Always have."

At the mention of 'ghosties', Ethan stared at me, his expression not betraying the disappointment he felt in my attitudes. It was another wedge between us, one I couldn't hide any longer. Would he accept that we saw the world in different ways or not?

Nevertheless, Erin had revealed her true colours and they weren't pretty ones. I suspected that undercurrent of hostility but not to this extent.

"And yet, here you are. Industrial espionage, breaking and entering, but the icing on the

153

cheesecake for you Erin, is poisoning. The procurator fiscal takes a dim view of Offences Against the Person Act."

It was an arguable point as she hadn't given me the green tablet directly but her lies meant she was responsible for my deranged behaviour yesterday. The words she called me weren't ones for Ava to hear.

"What should we do with her, Mr Davis?" the guard they called Wee Jimmy asked.

"Good question. This is a Castle therefore there's a dungeon or two. Perhaps there are a few rats left alive who'd welcome some company – and a snack?" He was joking, although Erin wasn't so sure.

"Rest assured, we'll find somewhere, Mr Davis. No one hurts Miss November like that." He produced a pair of handcuffs.

"What? You're not going to use those on me, you barbarian!"

"Don't worry, lassie. I'll wash them good and proper afterward." His mate sniggered.

Ethan wasn't quite finished with her though. "I want to try and understand, Erin. Why did you do it? Don't tell me it's for money?" No response. "Love then? Christian?"

This time he'd hit a nerve. "He loves me and he'll get me out of jail. Then we'll take the treasure and..."

Silly girl. She just confirmed there was treasure involved. The gems from the Netherlands robbery? We'd suspected of course once she reacted to Ava's declaration that she'd found valuables. We'd seen a few pieces she collected and put into her Treasure Chest. Erin wanted them. Ava found them outside, near the cotter's house.

Realising she'd said too much in her outburst,

Erin puffed up her considerable chest and declared she wasn't saying any more until she'd spoken to legal counsel.

"Christian doesn't like grasses. You didn't get anything from the sabotage guy, did you?

"That's true," Heather conceded. "Dead men don't talk. An accident in jail." She turned to Erin and added, "Hopefully, you'll have a longer life span in prison."

There was a pensive, subdued moment as Erin's face paled. Then she was cuffed and led away, head bowed.

◆　◆　◆　◆

We left Erin under guard to await the police's arrival. It was quite a relief. Ethan suggested we take a break outside in the sun.

"A constitutional, young Kirsty. I have my surprise to show you but, more crucially, we need to discuss that revelation about you seeing spirits of the dead."

He was holding my hand as we descended the steps to the Keep, heading towards the Lake of Mists. The trouble was I was uncertain if his tender grip was from affection or to simply steady me in my convalescence.

"I can explain."

I began wondering how to do that. The guy was a pragmatist; to him, the supernatural was solely for stories and reruns of Hammer horror films.

"No need to be defensive. Let's simply say I am changing my previously held dogmatic beliefs. I'm not saying I believe in phantoms with clanking chains yet but there is a presence here. I believe that Ava senses it and your gran certainly does. In addition, I confess that I intercepted that book

155

about Tillymoor that Lianne brought in for you. Interesting reading..."

By this time we were standing by the Lakeside. Our fingers were still intertwined. Ahead of us, damsel and dragonflies darted over the glistening blue waters that faded to grey as they approached that ubiquitous Mist.

"Is she here, now? This Grey Lady?"

I scanned the area. "No. Well, not that I can see. They... they have their own rules. Why the attitude change, sweetheart?"

"Little things... the book, chatting to your family, even Samantha and that voice she heard at night. I might have dismissed all of that had it not been for Ava telling us that the green tablet was bad. There's no logic to her and Heather knowing that. You talk to rain, see spectres and, not to put too fine a point on it, you've turned my life topsy-turvy. But I love you so much. I suspect that life with you by my side will be full of surprises."

"Talking of surprises...?"

"Oh yes. Come with me."

He paused for a second to make a phone call. Then, with an enigmatic smile, he led me to the rear of the Castle. I realised that I'd not been around here since my return from hospital. Nor had I been in any room facing the rear. Rounding the corner of the parking lot, I understood why.

Moira and the other office staff were filing out of the Annexe, Heather and Ava there as well.

"Goodness," I gasped, putting my knuckles to my lips. "What have you done, Ethan?"

He beamed as he led me and the others to the rear of the lot and up stairs to the Maze.

"What you suggested, kitten."

Then, turning to address the assembled throng. "Ladies, gentlemen and not forgetting my daughter, Ava. May I present for your recreation and enjoyment, the Tillymoor Maze, fully restored to its former glory. And this is not just for you. Bring your friends and families, after work, weekends, whenever. The townsfolk and tourists will be welcome too, to picnic, explore, and there's a creek over there suitable for bathing, boating or fishing, so I'm told. Just down there." He pointed.

Cheers and claps from everyone.

Ethan continued, "What are you waiting for? There's an early finish to all work at Tillymoor today and our caterers should be arriving momentarily with a picnic spread for everyone. Go on and explore the Maze. Try not to get lost!"

My colleagues didn't need to be asked twice. Even Moira chose to indulge her younger self, accompanying Heather and Ava.

"But how?" I asked Ethan, throwing my arms around to reach up and kiss his cheek.

"Just considered what you said. No feasibility study or costings, and there was a landscape gardening team on hold for a week at Kelso. It seemed a shame not to employ their talents."

"It looks absolutely gorgeous. But the plans?"

"In that book Lianne brought in. Plus her grandfather was Head Gardener here forty-odd years ago before the place fell into ruin."

"Shall we?" I said, with a skip and pirouette.

"If you insist," he replied.

"Our very own maze. How a-maz-ing is that?"

◆　　◆　　◆　　◆

DI Woolf had formally arrested Erin and reported back later by phone. Our songbird had waived her right to remain silent and was happily singing her heart out. One query was answered straight away, the reason she was injured by an explosive device planted by her criminal colleague was that the computer had blown up early. She told the police that it was meant to detonate at night as Christian didn't want innocents injured. Once it was pointed out that Mr Jenkins and Brodie – Christian's accomplices – were murdered, she admitted her gullibility. He'd told her they died accidentally. He'd lied.

From what Erin was privy to, Christian and his two accomplices had stolen the precious stones and gold over a year ago. The goods were smuggled into the UK and hidden until Interpol and other authorities eased off on their search. The two men were killed in a car accident not far from Gretna.

They'd arranged the delivery to a Scottish building firm as part of a consignment but they died before sharing details with Christian and intercepting the crate. Naturally Christian, the remaining thief, was distraught. All of his hard work in planning the robbery and safely smuggling the goods into the country was wasted. He spent weeks trying to locate the crate and secreted precious items. In the meantime, he ingratiated himself into the firm's ailing finances to be better positioned for locating the goods.

Erin hadn't any idea if the bulk of the stolen pieces were in the Castle or not, only that some were, she hoped, in Ava's room. Hence the break-in. Since Christian's other monies were frozen in his accounts, he was desperate to locate the stones and jewellery.

None of us had explored the older parts of the Castle. Consequently, they might be stashed anywhere, especially in the untouched parts of the ancient building. The tunnel beneath the wall was a shock, one that was unsuspected. Heaven knows what other hidden mysteries there were on the sealed upper floors. Again, it was logical to assume that Christian had the old Castle plans, the ones deleted from computer records.

When DI Woolf had finished, Ethan put down the phone which was on loud-speaker. Ava was reading in the adjoining room, glass doors separating us.

We'd never discover how the treasures, even a few of them, ended up in Tillymoor. Brought here accidentally in a crate marked Transudes with materials for the Castle renovation? Or possibly deliberately to be hidden by the accomplices who'd died?

What we were certain of was that, with Erin under lock and key, Christian would need to resort to doing his own dirty work.

I spoke to Gran on the phone. "They have enough to arrest him, Kirsty," she reassured me. "The sooner, the better. Providing round-the-clock protection from my agency isn't cheap, Shannon and your mum are safe and I have two guys in the house with me. I chose the best-looking ones. Even an old woman can have daydreams!"

◆　　◆　　◆　　◆

In retrospect, I wished Gran hadn't said the word 'dream'. My sleep that night wasn't the best. I was back with Mary Elizabeth, experiencing her life through my senses. I was there in her mind, feeling her hunger and pain. Frustration too, that I was a prisoner at Tillymoor in my windowless cell. I no longer was permitted even a glimpse of daylight save when I was led down the stairs to the outside at dusk. My eyes were too accustomed to the Stygian blackness of my hell-hole for me to emerge in full daylight, even in the cold winter.

There were fewer and fewer times that I appeared on parade at a ball, with threats that I should behave and smile sweetly. The Laird, always guiding me as he ambled between guests, made various excuses about my health when my gauntness and sunken eyes were commented upon. And if suspicions were there, nothing was uttered for fear that his rage and revenge be visited upon their families. After all, despite being the wife of the Laird, I was a nothing in their eyes, merely a a possession by law without any rights.

The outside walks around my pathway were reduced to weekly, not that I could count the days in that dismal place. I asked my turnkey which day and he told me. Whether it was the truth or not, I had no way of ascertaining.

The lake was frozen as I emerged, praying that I'd espy my gardener. Sadly, he was absent again though another was there.

"Where is Hector?" I whispered as my turnkey wandered off momentarily to relieve himself.

"Gone, my Lady. The master thought him overly familiar with thee. Dead or banished, we know not."

I sank to the damp grass wailing in pain and despair. There was nothing in my life, my last glimmer of light stolen from me.

Then I awoke, brow damp with perspiration. No wonder the Lady Mary Elizabeth drowned herself.

◆　　◆　　◆　　◆

Over the following days, life at Transudes gradually returned to normal. The same was true for me. Although I was eager to move back to my home, Shannon and Mum were caring for my cat, Fluff, and both Heather and Ethan insisted I stay until I was one hundred per cent.

Putting the lost weight back on was difficult and there was more than one attempt for me to have further tests. Rat Bite Fever was a mysterious disease in British medicine. Interactions with the drugs given by Christian and Erin was a possibility too. Nevertheless, I was working in my office for most of the day. Driving was aggravatingly out of the question but, when no one was looking, I'd go outside to sit in it and wallow in my company car's luxury.

To the surprise of all, Ethan's father, Kilmain Rhys-Davis, had fronted up to the police about his involvement with the 'she-wolf' himself, Christian Wilczyca. He attempted to make it right for Transudes as he absolved the company completely. Given the situation, his reputation was sullied and he stood down from all directorships immediately. Prison was unlikely as he had proof that he'd been coerced into any shady arrangements.

Christian, on the other hand, was implicated right up to his bushy black eyebrows. The story in the paper had the headline *Master Criminal on the Run*, ad in smaller print *Avoids Police Raid by Minutes*.

DI Woolf briefed us that .cut off from his dodgy bank accounts, Christian was a wanted felon without money. The stolen goods from Amsterdam were his sole chance of fleeing the country. He believed they were in the Castle or thereabouts. Perhaps they'd been smuggled in during or after the partial renovation, via the tunnel that was a secret entrance from olden days.

The Detective Inspector suggested stronger

security however Ethan thought we had enough.

Ava and I were getting on well although it was difficult to spend as much time as she wanted, playing games during these school holidays. I suggested that she have friends over but their parents weren't permitting that. The finding of Brodie's body and Tillymoor's reputation as a haunted Castle tended to dissuade them.

There weren't any further apparitions for any of us. How could we guess that it was just the lull before the storm?

◆　　◆　　◆　　◆

Moira came to apologise for Erin although she needn't. No one blamed her but, even so, she was determined to insist that a good manager should have noticed. Erin was a born liar. That wasn't even her real name. She'd fooled me and I was suspicious by nature. That conversation convinced me to take a proactive role in addressing each of the Departments at Transudes about the events which had taken place. Everyone deserved to be included in the truth behind the events that had put lives in peril. Ethan's father and his newspaper notoriety over the days fuelled rumour about Transudes and that wasn't acceptable with our employees.

Virtually none of the staff had visited the interior of Tillymoor Castle, solely Department Heads. It was an 'us versus them' scenario. That had to change and I was the person to do it. Caterers were called in and e-mail directives sent out, personal invitations from Ethan to attend a celebratory meeting in the Great Hall. From now on all such meetings would be in the Castle.

Accounts were first, not because of alphabetical

elitism (which I deplored) but because they were the ones most intimately affected by Erin's betrayal and the explosives. More importantly, they were my friends and colleagues. If I couldn't engage with them, then the day would be a pointless exercise.

The buffet was in place with instructions that it should be replenished for the subsequent hourly meetings. The waitresses and waiters would be called when needed. I was nervous.

"You can do this, Kirsty," Ethan encouraged me in between kisses. No lipstick today or attempts to cover up what had happened to me. This was a 'warts and all' revelation. No subject was taboo.

The doors opened and my audience filed in, awed at the grandeur of the original room, now resplendent in its restoration. Technically it was our audience but apart from the introduction and back-up for technical issues, I was the one leading this.

"Please take your seats, ladies and gentleman." That brought a subdued laugh, possibly from apprehension. Bruce was there to explain his findings and actions. Ethan apologised that he hadn't introduced himself in person earlier.

"Very remiss of me. When I first met Miss November, she had no idea that I'm your CEO. Talk about a sobering and quite soggy revelation."

More laughter, relaxed this time.

Ethan then continued with the announcement of the Megacity Contract with appropriate dramatic Powerpoint slides and music. The audience watched from the velvet-covered armchairs arranged in a semi-circle.

"Despite suffering from a disease called Rat Bite Fever, Miss November suggested improvements to the Megacity proposal that

163

secured our contract. This was on her second day as my SIC and justifies my controversial decision to appoint her. Since then, there have been other developments as she will tell you herself. I present, Miss Kirsty November."

The moment of truth. Would they accept me?

As I stood and before I could speak, Moira stood and began loudly clapping. My colleagues were on their feet too, joining in. So were Bruce and Ethan.

I urged them to sit. Start with a joke, Kirsty, I told myself.

"Thank you, everyone. Firstly, those reports of my death are slightly exaggerated." No one laughed but I noted a few tears. OK, too close to the truth. "But on the plus side, Rat Bite Fever diets do work."

A few smiles and genuine amusement this time. My confidence restored, I launched into a detailed fifteen-minute review of the history behind the murders, sabotage, then Erin's subversion and betrayal, and the latest on Christian.

"Are we safe here?" Lianne asked, voicing the concerns of most.

Ethan explained that both police and private security were on hand until the elusive Christian was found and arrested. That reassured them. Other queries were about me and my health. Also, ones about the ghostly figure many had seen, a woman in grey.

Interesting. I looked over to Ethan. We thought she'd vanished. Instead, she was manifesting to others. The question was why.

"Our Grey Lady ghost is nothing to be afraid of. Mary Elizabeth is a part of Tillymoor. Her statue is outside the keep, through which you entered earlier. She's been watching over us all. At this time, if there are no further questions, please mingle, enjoy the food and for the supernaturally inclined, there's a portrait of Mary Elizabeth on the wall over there."

He pointed. Yes, it was her, adorned in bright finery and jewels. "We had it restored. Transudes isn't simply about the future. Where practical, we honour the past. too."

"I didn't realise you had her portrait?"

"Neither did I. Ava told me it was her last night. When I asked, she said she just knew."

◆　　◆　　◆　　◆

Later DI Woolf called in person with distressing news. My family had been attacked in both their homes. Christian's henchmen. She assured me, saying that no one was injured. Gran's security had surprised and overpowered the intruders who confessed they were sent by Christian. He was desperate. They were the last of men loyal to him.

That left us as the remaining target. He was obsessional about retrieving the stolen Amsterdam valuables according to the individuals in custody. "His mind is totally donnart," one of the disgruntled prisoners confessed, angry that he was being charged for a crime that made no sense. The border-speak for someone stupid was a reminder of our strange expressions. For an inexplicable reason, he was fixated on me, angry that I'd humiliated him. He wasn't a lover of strong women, DI Woolf confirmed.

Ethan requested additional security. The situation with his father and Christian was a two-edged blade. Transudes was in the news and that saying by BT Barnum that any publicity was good publicity, strangely proved to be correct. We were the flavour of the moment with companies seeking our advice on expansion and building plans. Bruce was engaged to revamp the website as well.

Mum had been over to visit on several occasions, being made most welcome by Heather and Ava. I was more reticent. A lot of hurt needed to be released, although Gran and Mum had made up their differences. Could I be less gracious?

We discussed her abilities and how Dad had inexorably eroded her self-confidence. Their relationship became worse after I'd left home. As I suspected Dad was the driving force behind the split, blaming me and making out that he was an innocent bystander. When she learnt I was in the hospital, he refused to let her come visit. That led to her filing for divorce.

"Gran informed me that Mr Redcap is back."

"Yeah," I grinned, before becoming sombre. "All that time you spent convincing me he was a figment of my imagination and yet you could see him. It's not nice telling your daughter that she's seeing things."

"No. It's not. No excuses, Kirsty. I let a lot of people down."

We continued to talk though. That was important. Long-suppressed anger and tears could be shared at last. We agreed that she'd stay with me once I came home tomorrow. I had the space and we were committed to mending what had been broken. Being with Ethan, Ava and Heather reminded me that I'd been a recluse for too long.

Tonight would be my last in the Castle – that was until Ethan and I developed our relationship further...

The past few weeks on the roller-coaster of

dramas hadn't allowed us much of a chance, romantically speaking.

As to the special arrangements for my last evening at Tillymoor, I'm uncertain who suggested it. I was in the guest wing and therefore it made sense for it to be in my room. My pink bunny-rabbit pyjamas were off the agenda, a satin baby doll negligee my choice for the night. We were alone in the Castle as Heather had taken Ava to her place for the night. The prospect of seeing heather's new litter of puppies had been the ultimate enticement.

It was early for bedtime under other circumstances, not yet ten o'clock. Outside was a lazy summer evening and the setting sunlight streamed through the windows.

It seemed ages but the anticipation was worth it. He entered once I invited him in, a box of chocolates and flowers held out for me.

"Kirsty. You are absolutely stunning."

"Thank you, kind sir. But why the presents?"

"It's our first date," he explained.

"In a way, but not in the way that counts, but the chocolates are a lovely thought... for after. If you've brought gifts, I should give you mine now."

I slowly lifted the straps from my shoulders then let the nightie slither to the floor.

He stood entranced before approaching to embrace and kiss me. I revelled in his touch and the eagerness of what was to come.

Then, as I felt his warm breath grazing my ear lobes, the power went out.

"What the...?" Ethan backed away as the much dimmer emergency lighting kicked in. "Blackout. Outside lights are off. Where's my walkie-talkie?"

I didn't ask the reason he'd brought that with him to our special night – Ethan was Ethan – and he was concerned for us all and our security.

"Duncan...? Anyone...? Report! What's going on out there?" Nothing. Desperate, he tried again before grabbing my mobile. "No signal. That's impossible. The cell tower's close by. Someone must be jamming it."

The walkie-talkie buzzed.

"Duncan. Thank goodness. What's going–?"

"Sorry. Duncan's unable to answer right now."

Ethan's face showed shock. "Christian? What do you want?"

"My treasure, of course, Ethan. We're coming for it... and no one's going to stop us."

CHAPTER 15

Flustered, I asked, "What can we do?"

"I don't know. I can't concentrate with you like that. Christian caught us with our pants down – literally."

He was right. Madly, I scrambled through the drawers for my underwear then, on reflection, into slacks and a warm sweater.

Ethan kept trying the phone, to no avail.

"No use, Kirsty. He must be jamming mobile communication. He'll probably disable the emergency power next to stop the alarms and automatic police alert. He wants us scared and he's in no hurry." Then he noticed me. "Why are you dressed like a mountain climber?"

"We're hiding in the old parts of Tillymoor. Up above us. You get yourself and the others dressed like me. I'll get flashlights and the plans."

"Plans? What plans? There's no records of the higher floors or access to them. Christian wiped them from the systems."

168

By this time, we were running down towards Ava's and Heather's rooms. Panting already, it was difficult to explain. "Got them from the... surveyor... Transudes used before ... the build... the paper ones."

We parted then, promising to meet back in five. The emergency lighting remained on, thank goodness. I rushed to retrieve the Castle plans from my office and flashlights from the store cupboard. We occasionally needed them for inspecting partially completed projects. I picked up two of the fully-charged Xenon ones.

We met just as the remaining dim emergency lights flickered and went out.

Ethan's walkie talkie crackled. "We're coming for you, Ethan. Your sassy floosie too. Just tell us the location of my jewels."

He was about to answer but I put my hand on his. "Dump that radio, Ethan. If he hears his voice and you're carrying it, then he'll guess where we are. Better still, put it in the rubbish chute. That way he won't realise we've been here."

I was whispering, worried we might be overheard. No idea how he was breaking in but I suspected that underground tunnel. He could bash through the boarded-up door.

"Sorry, my love. We're on a surprise game of Hide and Seek and we have to be extra quiet."

Creeping into Ethan's office, we continued into the bathroom. I prayed Christian was a long way from us and wouldn't hear our shoes on the tiles.

"This is your grand plan? To hide in here?"

I hushed Ethan, pressing on the walls in turn until one section sprung open. "Access panel. Concealed hinges and flush fitting. The ducting, power and water pipes are behind there in the corridor so watch your head and feet. Low ceilings.

169

Turn right and up the stairs to the third level."

Transudes had done their magic on the lower two levels, not destroying the ancient structure but simply putting a facade of false walls over much of it. The third storey was structurally sound but left untouched. It extended over the entire structure whereas the fourth level was in the round turrets and keep. Although high, the windows were tiny, many of them balistrariae or arrow-loop openings. No glass in them so those parts would be cold.

My heart was thumping in a controlled panic. Christian had remorsefully killed people. He wanted 'his' treasure, and none of us had any idea where it was. Would he believe that? I doubted it. Logically, if we had found the stolen jewels and gold, they would have been given to the authorities and returned to their rightful owners. But Christian didn't behave in that way. He was a thief and figured that we'd discovered then kept the valuables for ourselves.

Consequently, we had to stay out of his clutches for as long as possible. Hiding was our sole option until help arrived. But no one was aware we were in trouble so the chance of the cavalry riding in at the last moment, bugles blaring, was low to zero.

"Where are we heading, Kirsty?" Ethan asked.

"Up. Second floor. Creepy spiders and dust."

"OK. After that?"

"I'm working on it."

It was good fortune that I'd studied the hand-drawn plans with annotations and discussed them with the surveyor. At least I had a mental picture. The third level of this castle was a rabbit warren of corridors and small rooms. Accommodation for the servants or guards perhaps?

Then I stopped.

Christian had the same plans as we did. We couldn't hide in the Castle. What had I been thinking? Instead, he'd search the place methodically until we were cornered like a you-know-what in a trap with no possibility of escape.

We needed a place he didn't have plans to.

"Forget my master escape plan, Ethan. Time for Plan B." I explained my rationale and headed down inside the false walls instead of up. With luck, we'd bypass one another, the modern façade separating us.

"Where to, Kirsty?"

"The one place we can hide outside that he doesn't know… the Maze."

It would be light for another hour and the Maze was extensive. At least two acres of intricate pathways with right angles, twists and dead ends. I had Lianne's book in my coat pocket, a lucky coincidence. It had an aerial plan. The hedges were all nine feet high and thick enough that you could be a yard away and not see a person on the other side.

Moving from the Castle to the Maze was the trickiest. We'd be exposed crossing the car park. Fingers crossed, our pursuers would be in the bowels of the building and not see us. Clambering up the steps was hard. They were steep, much steeper than modern landscaping would use.

"Hey! There they are!" someone shouted from the rear. We'd been spotted, possibly from a window. The voice was distant so we had a chance to outrun them.

A shot rang over our heads. Fragments of greenery sprayed everywhere. We redoubled our efforts. Given the distance, the gunshots couldn't be accurate. Another shot. Ethan grunted, staggering as he clasped his upper arm.

171

We reached the entrance to the Maze. It wasn't enough. Hedges aren't bulletproof. We had to get inside, deep inside and well out of sight.

"Stop, you idiot! I want them alive," Christian shouted to whoever had fired at us. "Get up there into that weird forest thing. Find them."

From the cover of the privet hedge, I studied our adversaries sprinting over the car park. Two were dressed as our guards. No wonder we'd been caught unawares. The third was Christian. We had to move deeper into the Maze.

Mazes and labyrinths were often used interchangeably but there was a difference. A labyrinth leads in one direction to the centre. Our maze had multiple exits and entrances. With the low sun and the high hedges about four feet apart, the pathway was bathed in bright sunlight and deep, dark shadows at our level. It took a moment for our eyes to adjust to the relative gloom. Taking Ethan's hand, I led us deep into the geometric puzzle. The closer to the outside, the more vulnerable we were.

They'd be struggling to navigate the Maze, but I had an edge. During the past few days, I'd indulged myself exploring in here. The pathways were meant to confuse, each one identical to others in length or right-angle turns.

But they weren't. Plus I had the drawn aerial plan. If we could weave our way through to the rear of the Lake of Mists then into the forest...

There was no point trying to drive off. Our cars would have been disabled. Christian wasn't about to take chances.

We stopped and I examined Ethan's arm. A flesh wound and not a lot of blood loss but he was in shock. Being shot was a new experience for him. He was dazed and not thinking clearly. I

172

bound the wound as well as I could with a clean linen pillowcase I'd grabbed to put the torches in. We couldn't make a sound. Ethan gritted his teeth as I tied a knot, not too tight as I didn't want to restrict the circulation.

Sadly my plan to hide in these passages had a flaw. In trimming back the overgrown plants, some parts of the hedges were bereft of foliage. In six months, the cover would be complete. We didn't have that length of time. Hell. We didn't have six hours before they caught us. The sound of a breaking twig, spying a flash of colour through the green... any slip-up could be our downfall.

Nighttime might help but at the moment I wouldn't have placed any bets on us surviving. Carefully, I rubbed mud over our clothes and exposed skin in between moving away from where they sounded to be. I stopped to check the map. Assuming I hadn't missed a turn, we were close to the Lake end of the forest.

A noise alerted us to another concern. It was mechanical and it was coming closer. I checked the phones; the reception was still non-existent. What was it? A mower? Then I glimpsed it through trees that surrounded the Maze.

"Damn it, Ethan – a drone!"

Who would have thought it; a spy in the sky? Looks as though they came prepared for anything. We had no chance. I could see the camera mounted forward of the four mini-helicopter blades. It was coming closer in a straight line as though following a search pattern.

Making sure we were in the shadows and to the side of the mechanical bird, I listened to it pass then peeked out. I grabbed a stone.

"What are you doing, Kirsty?" Ethan asked, wincing as he moved his arm.

"Champion pitcher in our girls' baseball team. Hope I've not lost my touch."

The almost stationary target was about twenty feet high and moving slowly away at an angle. By standing, I might have exposed our position. I hoped not.

The baseball-sized stone flew upwards, clipping a rotor. The drone wobbled and regained its course before that rotor exploded from the imbalance and the drone spiralled to crash some ten yards away.

A loving pat on my back from Ethan. "You killed it, lover."

"No cracks about throwing like a girl?" I wondered softly. He kissed me briefly as we moved on. By now, the gloaming shadows were cloaking us protectively, the sun almost set.

A wisp of mist appeared, then another.

"The Lake must be close," I cautioned.

We dared not use our torches but our night vision plus our sense of touch allowed us to lose ourselves deeper in the warren of passageways. Glancing back, flashes of moving torchlight appeared through the regimented bushes. Christian and his henchmen weren't concerned about using their flashlights even if they telegraphed their positions. It allowed them to move faster, intimidating us at the same time. Judging from Ethan's agitation, their tactics were succeeding.

Ethan and I almost tripped over one another onto the ground as creatures threw up their tiny arms in fright. They vanished immediately, not moving from the spot.

"Can't be rats," he said in hushed tones, holding me close. "They wore clothes."

"Dunters." I'd seen them once as a toddler.

Part of border folklore, they haunted castles.

"What? Do they exist? I thought they were made up stories to frighten kiddies."

"They're not naughty," I explained, "Just scared of humans. They're shy."

The noise from the intruders was closer, too close. It was as though he was tracking us somehow. Then I realised, having lost their drone, they'd resorted to heat sensors or night-vision glasses. They'd locked onto our body heat. There was no escaping them now.

CHAPTER 16

Suddenly the truth hit me. Ethan and I had spied the Dunters. We were within feet of the Lake of Mists. I sensed it in the air. There was magic here too, an ancient magic drawing power from the surroundings. Taking a deep breath, I closed my eyes and stood up defiantly.

Ethan was frantic. He grabbed my hand to pull me down to his crouching position. "What are you doing, Kirsty? They'll see us!"

"Time to stop running, lover. Trust me."

My words were to reassure him but I was scared. What if my plan failed? By the time the three armed men rounded a corner of the Maze to illuminate us with their flashlights, my hushed requests to the raindrops were in the air.

At first, there was no change.

"Come on, guys. I need you," I whispered.

At last, tenuous ribbons of fog flowed around Ethan and me, swirling slowly like a placid whirlwind playing games. The droplets coalesced into a shield forming a reflective fog that blinded our attackers momentarily.

175

They swung their torches to avert their lights.

The Lake of Mists was expanding as more water droplets evaporated from the surface. The hoar became thicker, so dense in places that we couldn't see our hands before our faces. Then there was the cold, drawing energy from the bodies of Christian and his colleagues, yet leaving us inviolate.

The sound came next, or rather the absence of it... They began to panic, unable to see, doubled up as the frigidity seeped into the very centre of their souls.

"Run!" I called out and they did – all but Christian.

His willpower was formidable and my capabilities to control the rain droplets was ebbing fast. The fog dissipated as quickly as it came. Ethan went to subdue Christian before he regained his composure, though it was too late. He shoved Ethan to one side before levelling his gun at me.

"Don't know what you did, lady, but you won't be doing it again."

Suddenly, from out of the Mists, the spirit of Mary Elizabeth appeared. She was soaking and running from the Lake. She hadn't drowned after all. Dashing by us, I sensed she was escaping to meet with her true love, Hector.

Christian and Ethan witnessed her flight but Christian chose to block her path.

But she was a ghost, an echo from times long since passed, She ran through him as though he wasn't there and into the Maze – and her release from the Laird's control over her life.

She was free.

As for Christian, he knelt on the bare, damp soil, a whimper escaping his lips every so often.

Ethan grabbed his weapon and dragged him to his feet. At last, it was over.

"Are you OK, lover?" he asked, hugging me.

"Yeah, weak as a kitten but yeah... alright."

"You were incredible, Kirsty. Pity you look such a mess with all that gunge and dirt you smeared on us, otherwise, I might kiss you. What the hell. I'll do it anyway."

Once he did, we had to rest against the hedge. Both of us were drained. Finally, Ethan pushed himself to his feet and switched on his torch. Christian wasn't going anywhere.

"What I just saw... what you did. It was..." He didn't finish the sentence. It was too overwhelming. "You truly do talk to the rain? I realise you said that the day I first met you but... what's it like?"

I managed a wan smile. "Hard. Well, hard to do what I did. It's this place that helped. I doubt I could do it again, even now. Haven't you noticed? The mist is gone." That magical ambience too.

"Hey, you're right. Guess we'll have to rename the Lake. How does Mary's Lake sound?"

I took his hand to kiss it. "Perfect. I'm certain that she'd approve. You felt it, didn't you? Her spirit's no longer tied to Tillymoor. I hope wherever she escaped to, her life was better."

"I pray it was, too."

He rubbed his arm gingerly. The pain was more noticeable as the adrenalin rush left him.

"Reckon, it's time to leave this Maze. It saved our lives, you realise, along with you and – I don't believe I'm saying it – a ghost." He flashed the torch all around us. "You *can* get us out of here, can't you?"

"Sure. It's just down here on the left." I turned

to get my bearings. "Or maybe the right…" I chewed my lip. "No. Definitely left at the next T-junction. Trust me, lover."

◆　◆　◆　◆

It was quite a while before we exited the Maze.

Three police cars and a helicopter, sirens blaring and lights flashing, came into view as we Irydid so. Talk about the cavar *not* arriving in the nick of time!

DI Woolf led Christian away. We'd been lucky, as Gran suggested it was a brief touching with Tillymoor's past saving us in the present.

At last, the dramas were over for us – and for Mary Elizabeth. I hugged Ethan as we made our way back to the ambulances.

Another stay in the hospital for me, I expected. An overnight stay as Ethan's gunshot wound was assessed as superficial. But perhaps they'd give us adjoining rooms.

CHAPTER 17

Tomorrow is the first anniversary of that night. It's also our wedding day.

Ethan, Ava and I are seated under the showers as the sun sets, admiring the reflections and dancing dragonflies over the water. The mists are gone. They vanished the night that Christian and the remnants of his organisation were imprisoned.

The officers who had arrived captured the traitorous security personnel, the ones who'd intercepted and tied Duncan up so that he couldn't intervene.

The trouble was that Duncan had a few tricks of his own and, accepting that he was outnumbered, had trekked to the nearest farmhouse to raise the alarm.

Christian has not been the same since that evening. He insists he saw a ghost and that it attacked him. The doctors put his imaginings down to a traumatic experience, shaking their heads and declaring that his mind will probably never recover.

Now, Ava is enjoying the rain soaking her. She's chosen to adopt my idiosyncrasies. Ethan hasn't – at least not yet – he has his open umbrella and rain jacket on.

"Are you certain tomorrow will be warm, sunny and dry, Kirsty? They're forecasting rain all over Scotland."

"Trust me, lover. Friends in high places. The advantage of being a Rain Whisperer."

He accepts my word. Ethan's so lovely and open-minded, like that. The rain is cool on my face yet very refreshing. I sigh. "Penny for your thoughts, sweetheart?"

"Just thinking of Mary. We have her blessing, you know. I just hope our lives together will be as good as hers eventually was.

As Christian suspected, the stolen goods from the Netherlands robbery were in the upper reaches of the Castle. There was an opened Transudes crate on one of the floors but the treasure had been hidden in the turret cell where Mary had lived.

The police thought it was the thief, I was convinced it was the Dunters.

Along with the items in Ava's cracker box, everything was accounted for and returned to the authorities in Amsterdam. The story made the

179

news and once more, gave Transudes a boost publicity-wise.

While the police were retrieving the stolen goods, they discovered a letter from Mary on vellum. It was secreted behind a loose stone in the turret walls. It had been very coincidental to find it then, but I'd given up trying to second guess the ancestral connection and timeslip link between us.

The translation from Latin told us the story after she had swam to her freedom. She ran off with Hector to a full, loving life. Years later she returned to Tillymoor after the Laird had passed away. From her accounts, he died a broken man.

♦   ♦   ♦   ♦

I hear Mum's bus arriving. She's happy to buy my house as the divorce from Dad is now final. We're getting on well together, making up for all those lost years. Even now, with me living in the Castle, we meet regularly. Tonight is one of those nights. Tillymoor Haunted Castle and Maze Tours are doing well for her.

No more ghosts as such, since the Grey Lady has never been seen since that evening, Nevertheless we do have a few surprises for the paying clients visiting us. Transudes is very successful as a modern, progressive company but using the original, untouched part of Tillymoor Castle to pay homage to its history works very well too.

"Time to go," I remind them Ethan and Ava now. It's a big day tomorrow.

"You guys, too. It's showtime," I call to the wee folk who'd joined us at the water's edge.

The five-inch high Shellycoats, Dunters and

Redcaps scamper gleefully back to Tillymoor Castle. They're ready to provide the arriving 'ghost tour' clients with enough frights to give them their money's worth. And the gossamer-winged fairies plus other fae folk in the Maze will give the visiting kiddies so much delight.

Of course, the explanations for the doubters in the bus tour are that of holograms and elaborate special effects. That way everyone leaves Tillymoor happy.

I take one more glance around the estate, the scent of night jasmine filling the air. Then I clasp Ava's hand tightly. There's a very large puddle in front of us. Ethan grimaces and reluctantly takes my other hand in his.

"Are you sure about this, Kirsty?"

The puddle is far too tempting.

"Shall we or not?" I ask them.

They both nod.

Ethan bends his legs and starts the countdown. "Three... two... one..."

Puzzle Pages

PUZZLES ANSWERS TURN TO PAGE 190

Put your mental agility to the test with our selection of fiendishly fun brain teasers…

Sudoku

Fill in each of the blank squares with the numbers 1 to 9, so that each row, each column and each 3x3 cell contain all the numbers 1 to 9.

		6			7			
		2		1		4	7	
3	4		5				9	
		8			1			
	9					3		
7			2		6	1		
	2			8	9			
	1	3					2	9
							3	8

Word Wheel

You have 10 minutes to find as many words as possible using the letters in the wheel. Each word must be three letters or more and contain the central letter. Use each letter once and no plurals, foreign words or proper nouns are allowed. There is at least one 9-letter word.

Average: 13 words Good: 14-19 words Excellent: 20-25 words

Puzzler

183

Missing Link

The answer to each clue is a word which has a link with each of the three words listed. This word may come at the end (eg HEAD linked with BEACH, BIG, HAMMER), at the beginning (eg BLACK linked with BEAUTY, BOARD and JACK) or a mixture of the two (eg STONE linked with HAIL, LIME and WALL).

ACROSS

1 Bomb, Building, Manager (4)
3 General, Hall, Welsh (8)
8 Ball, Head, Hut (5)
9 Gang, Gutter, Printing (5)
11 Aunt, Coat, Dane (5)
12 Games, Record, Village (7)
14 Bus, War, Well (4)
16 Along, Car, Sea (4)
20 Imaging, Printer, Underwear (7)
22 Angle, Down, Forth (5)
24 Back, Rind, Streaky (5)
26 Good, Lost, Way (5)
27 Compound, Human, Rate (8)
28 Awake, Calm, Put (4)

DOWN

1 Bag, Cake, Finger (6)
2 Bird, Manners, Tennis (5)
4 Charm, Finishing, Old (6)
5 Handed, Stomach, Threat (5)
6 Bumble, Keeper, Line (3)
7 Bouncy, New, Sand (6)
10 Cloth, Knap, Race (4)
13 Bachelor, Key, Launch (3)
15 Golden, Group, Ice (3)
16 Bean, Brussels, Wings (6)
17 Cheque, Cigarette, Pencil (4)
18 Brake, Building, Starting (6)
19 Fingers, Situation, Wicket (6)
21 Asia, Key, Planet (5)
23 Appearance, Celebrity, House (5)
25 Burglar, Flap, Nap (3)

SOLUTIONS ON PAGE 190

My Weekly

ON SALE EVERY TUESDAY

YOUR FEEL GOOD READ!

10 Ways Christmas Is Good For You!

£1.00

My Weekly

Chocolate Delights!

Icelandic Adventure

PLUS

Fabulous Festive Food

Tina O'Brien

"It's nice to put down roots"

Get Cosy!

Warm and Welcoming Homes

Snuggly Fashion

EXCLUSIVE! Milly Johnson Story

There's something for everyone!

Fiction, Celebs, Health, Travel, Puzzles

Kriss Kross

Fit the words below into the Kriss Kross grid.

4 letters	6 letters	8 letters	10 letters
Adze	Ambler	Oratorio	Alternator
Honk	Careen	Surmount	Transverse
Lilo			
Nest	7 letters	9 letters	11 letters
	Aseptic	Essential	Adolescence
5 letters	Empress	Idiomatic	Cleanliness
Earth			
Stake			

Codebreaker

Each letter of the alphabet has been replaced by a number.
Work out which number represents which letter in the grid.
We've given you the first three to get you started.

16		22		8				25		11		10
6	15	15	25	10	9		6	19	4	2	19	1
15		12		11		17		6		14		20
10	5	18	2	10	6	19	18	9		14	6	2
5		2		12		1						26
21	10	11	8	7	7	12	15	1		26	19	18
		15		19		10		11		15		
15	12	1		1	2	8	6	19	5	10	18	15
3						8		14		26		12
21	7	18		8	6	15	12	18	15	7	2	26
7		7				11		19		12		2
11	2	24	8	2	26		26	12	15	15	13	15
18		16		11				23		1		1

A B C̶ D E F G H I̶ J K L̶ M N O P Q R S T U V W X Y Z

1	2	3	4	5	6	7	8	9	10	11	12	13
				C	L							
14	15	16	17	18	19	20	21	22	23	24	25	26
					I							

SOLUTIONS ON PAGE 190

Now Monthly

Solutions To Puzzles

SOLUTION TO SUDOKU

1	8	6	9	4	7	2	5	3
9	5	2	8	1	3	4	7	6
3	4	7	5	6	2	8	9	1
5	6	8	7	3	1	9	4	2
2	9	1	4	5	8	3	6	7
7	3	4	2	9	6	1	8	5
6	2	5	3	8	9	7	1	4
8	1	3	6	7	4	5	2	9
4	7	9	1	2	5	6	3	8

KRISS KROSS

SOLUTION TO MISSING LINK

ACROSS: 1 Site 3 Assembly 8 Beach 9 Press 11 Great 12 Olympic 14 Fare 16 Side 20 Thermal 22 Right 24 Bacon 26 Cause 27 Interest 28 Stay
DOWN: 1 Sponge 2 Table 4 School 5 Empty 6 Bee 7 Castle 10 Sack 13 Pad 15 Age 16 Sprout 17 Stub 18 Blocks 19 Sticky 21 Minor 23 Guest 25 Cat
SHADED WORD: YEOMEN

WORD WHEEL

Solution: BUTTERFLY

CODEBREAKER

Could YOU write a Pocket Novel?

We believe EVERYONE has a story in them, and we would love to read yours!

Five Steps To Writing A Thrilling Good Read

1. Imagine your heroine…
2. Add the charismatic man of your dreams…
3. Pitch them together in a mystery or romance…
4. Obstacles and adventures abound…
5. All is overcome for our happy ending!

Where and When

Stories can be set in any place, in any era
Who Create believable characters so we care…
What Happens to them!
How Write the first three chapters and send them along with a synopsis of your plot to **myweekly@dcthomson.co.uk**
Length: 50,000 words

191

ORDER FORM

Please complete the coupon below and send it to:

**My Weekly Subscriptions, DC Thomson Shop,
PO Box 766, Haywards Heath, RH16 9GF**

YES, I would like to subscribe to **MY WEEKLY POCKET NOVELS** for:

❏ **BEST DEAL!** Only £6 for your first 6 issues then £13 every 3 months (UK) by direct debit*
❏ 1 year for £50 (UK) or £80 (Overseas) by cheque
❏ 2 years for £86.40 (UK) or £144 (Overseas) by cheque

Your Details

Title .... Name.. Address ....
....Postcode ....

Telephone...Email ....

Delivery Details (If different from above)

Title .... Name...Address ....
....Postcode ....

1. DIRECT DEBIT

⬤ **DIRECT Debit**

INSTRUCTIONS TO YOUR BANK/BUILDING SOCIETY
TO PAY BY DIRECT DEBIT

Originator's Identification Number

3	8	8	5	5	2

Name and full postal address of your Bank or Building Society

To the Manager	Bank/Building Society
Address	
	Postcode

Instruction to your Bank or Building Society
Please pay DC Thomson & Co Ltd Direct debit from the account detailed in this instruction subject to the safeguards assured by the Direct Debit Guarantee. I understand that this instruction may remain with DC Thomson & Co Ltd and if so, details will be passed electronically to my Bank/Building society.

Signature(s)

Name(s) of A/c Holder(s)

FOR DC THOMSON & CO LTD OFFICIAL USE ONLY
This is not part of the instruction to your Bank or Building society.

Bank/Building Account No

Branch Sort Code

Bank and Building Societies may not accept
Direct Debits for some types of account

2. CHEQUE

I enclose my cheque (no cash please) for:
made payable to **DC Thomson & Co Ltd**   £